VERTICAL WORLD ∀

A NEW FAMILY

BY BRIAN CRAWFORD

EPIC Escape

An Imprint of EPIC Press
abdopublishing.com

A New Family
Vertical World: Book #6

abdopublishing.com

Published by EPIC Press, a division of ABDO, PO Box 398166, Minneapolis, Minnesota 55439. Copyright © 2019 by Abdo Consulting Group, Inc. International copyrights reserved in all countries. No part of this book may be reproduced in any form without written permission from the publisher. Escape™ is a trademark and logo of EPIC Press.

Printed in the United States of America, North Mankato, Minnesota.
052018
092018

♻

Cover design by Christina Doffing
Images for cover art obtained from iStockphoto.com
Edited by Gil Conrad

Library of Congress Cataloging-in-Publication Data

Library of Congress Control Number: 2018932906

Publisher's Cataloging in Publication Data

Names: Crawford, Brian, author.
Title: A new family/ by Brian Crawford
Description: Minneapolis, MN : EPIC Press, 2019 | Series: Vertical world; #6
Summary: Ætherian operatives swarm Cthonia, so the Cthonians, Rex, Máire, and Aral flee, but they are soon embroiled in a firefight with an advance Ætherian guard. When the Cthonians defeat the Ætherians, they force the sky dwellers to remove their respirators. Realizing the air on Cthonia is breathable, the Ætherians join with the Cthonians to tell the remaining Ætherians above the truth about Cthonia. A revolution begins.
Identifiers: ISBN 9781680769166 (lib. bdg.) | ISBN 9781680769449 (ebook)
Subjects: LCSH: Secret operations--Fiction. | Survival--Fiction--Fiction. | Revolutions--Fiction--Fiction. | Science fiction--Societies, etc--Fiction | Young adult fiction.
Classification: DDC [FIC]--dc23

This series is dedicated to Debbie Pearson.
Thank you for everything.

ONE

WHEN REX RAN FROM THE GROUNDED AIR-
ship, everyone froze.

The Cthonian spotters stopped cataloguing their bodies. Tom lifted his eyes from the rubble. Máire let Franklin Strapp's Tracker fall to the ground with a broken-sounding *clump*. Behind them, the debris continued to smolder, but the Cthonians who'd been searching the wreckage stood like statues as two Ætherians reunited in their midst.

"Mom!" Rex screamed, his eyes fixed on Máire Himmel, who turned to face him. To Máire's left, Tom looked back and forth between the two, confused. Some of the soldiers fidgeted with their weapons, not sure if they should stop Rex or let him be. Like most people in Cthonia, they'd all heard of him; they all knew Máire's story. Their eyes darted from Rex to Máire to Tom. They especially kept their eyes on their expedition leader for his reaction. But he too seemed to be processing what was happening.

It was only when a body smacked into the ground at three hundred miles per hour that the Cthonians sprang to life. Whoever it was had just fallen from somewhere in Ætheria. Someone had been Tossed.

"Ah!" Rex shouted at the impact, jumping back in horror and covering his face with his uninjured arm. Máire turned away and brought her hands above her head as if expecting something else to fall.

"What is that?!" Tom snapped. "What is it?!"

A dozen of the Cthonian soldiers rushed in, half of them pointing their guns at the body, half keeping their guns trained toward the sky, as if ready to shoot down any more falling objects. Some of them stepped up and surrounded the impact site, while the others kept their rifles pointed upward. Tom approached the body, kneeling to turn it over. Rex peered through the line of Cthonians for a better look.

There, lying in the center of a six-foot-long, oval crater, Rex saw the uniform of an ACF Protector. Amid the dust and the agitated Cthonians who were moving about, he at first couldn't make out who it was. But when he saw that it was Challies, his breath failed him. Amid the terror of nearly being killed, the contradictory emotions of having found his mother and the realization that the last Ætherian to help him was now dead, Rex's mind became numb and empty. It was as if the overwhelming power of all of these feelings canceled each other out, leaving him to be little more than a hollow shell. He felt nothing. He heard nothing. Even the pain from his relocated shoulder vanished in a swirl of delirium. And even though he could still register the Cthonians frenetically working to examine the body for clues that could help them make sense of everything that had been happening, Rex was not aware of what he was actually seeing.

"Rex?" Máire muttered tentatively.

He didn't respond.

She stepped up and placed her hand on his uninjured shoulder.

"Rex?"

Startled, Rex turned toward her, his face expressionless. Despite the commotion around them, the two gazed at each other silently, as if in a dream.

While he stood facing her, Máire scanned Rex's face for signs she might recognize in this sixteen-year-old boy. When she'd last seen him as a newborn, his right eye drooped and the right side of his mouth had remained paralyzed. When he'd smiled or cooed, he'd always smiled only from the left side of his face. Even when nursing, the right side of Rex's face almost never moved, and milk dribbled down his chin and into the folds of his neck. While working in Cthonia, Máire often thought about how her growing son would deal with his handicap—or even if he'd survived past childhood. She often spoke about him to anyone in the Cthonian Cave Complex who would listen.

"Rex? Is it you?" she muttered, her lip trembling. She saw instantly that his right eye seemed lazy and his mouth crooked. Still, she'd grown so used to protecting herself from hoping too much over the past years that part of her didn't want to believe what she was seeing. *What if this was just another Ætherian with the same deformity? What if the Head Ductor is playing some sort of cruel joke on me, just to make me suffer even more? What if . . .*

As if startled from a trance, Rex's eyes suddenly focused on his mother's eyes. Wary, he stepped back from her, holding out his left hand for her to stay back.

An awkward tension enveloped the two. Behind them, the Cthonians had finished their preliminary survey of the body and stood. While some of the soldiers kept their eyes skyward, the others watched the two in silence, rapt. Like Rex, they too felt numbed by everything that was unfolding so quickly.

Moving like someone who'd been drugged, Rex slid his unwounded hand into his AG suit and pulled out the photograph he'd taken from his foster dad's cabinet. It was still there—folded, but intact. This was the same image he'd shown to Aral when they'd first met—this was what had allowed his Unit Alif to trust her so quickly, and this was what gave his life a new direction: to find his mother. More importantly, this was the only image he'd ever seen of his mother since infancy.

Now, as all watched, Rex unfolded the small picture, but didn't look at it. Instead, he kept his eyes on the woman standing in front of him, her feet planted in the wreckage of where his foster dad had worked and died. He lifted the photo and held it at arm's length so that, in his line of vision, the image was next to Máire's actual face. His eyes jumped between the two like a painter comparing his work to the subject.

And then he recognized her.

Despite the trauma of Challies's body landing near them, an unfamiliar warmth began to take root deep in his chest and expand to all of his limbs. Máire sensed his recognition, and before he could say anything or react, she cried out, jumping forward with her arms outstretched. She'd known it was him from her first glimpse of his face. But she somehow felt she needed his approval—his acceptance—to embrace her son.

With his nerves already on edge from everything he'd experienced over the past weeks, Rex jumped back in alarm, his hands jumping up to protect himself. Around him, the Cthonian spotters seemed unsure what to do: Hold Máire back? Offer support? Say something? In their confusion, they did and said nothing.

Meanwhile, back in the airship, Aral emerged from her hiding place and stood in the open door, watching the scene unfold. Because they were all watching the bizarre family reunion unfold in front of them, none of the Cthonians noticed her. Seeing that Rex had finally found what he was looking for, Aral allowed a smile to cross her face.

"Rex! Rex, it's you! Oh, my God! Rex, my baby, my baby boy!" Máire threw her arms around her sixteen-year-old son and squeezed. Since she'd left Ætheria so long ago, this was the first time she'd embraced another human being. Having been traumatized by the Head Ductor's expelling her, having to abandon her baby son, and having to integrate into the new and strange world of Cthonia, she'd spent the past sixteen years withdrawn into herself—doing her work, talking only when necessary, but also rambling on and on about her lost, disfigured son.

As she squeezed, she breathed in deeply, trying to recall long-lost smells she'd forgotten over the years. Gone were the powdery smells of diapers, creams, and baby toys that she'd left Rex with. Instead, her nostrils inhaled the musky, sweaty body odor of a young man.

"Rex, Rex, Rex . . . " she muttered, turning her head to kiss her son on the cheek. "Rex . . . "

"Stop!" Tom shouted, as if suddenly snapping awake and realizing the implications of what he was seeing. He had a duty, after all, and he couldn't let his emotions blind him to his mission. He stepped toward the two. He clutched his firearm with both hands, his eyes boring into Rex. Ignoring Máire, he examined Rex head to toe, his face filled with suspicion.

"Ætherian!" Tom spat, his words venomous. "How did you get here? When? Were you here six days ago? On eqūs with other Ætherians? Put your hand on your head!"

Dumbstruck, Rex complied. He lifted his left hand to the top of his head. As he did, the photograph slipped from his grasp and wafted to the ground. Tom nodded to another Cthonian, who stepped up to Rex and patted him down, searching

for weapons. Rex glanced at his name patch:
HECTOR.

"A group of Ætherians attacked our airship. Last Thursday. Were you part of that group? How long have you been down here?! Tell me!"

At the angry Cthonian's demands, Rex felt a tingling sensation of dread spread from his chest to his arms and legs. Images and sounds of the firefight in which Yoné had been killed flooded his mind. How could he escape from the Ætherians, only to be captured by the Cthonians? What would they do to him if they thought he'd been in the group that had attacked them? He hadn't fired at them on purpose, but this Cthonian didn't know that. After all, the airship had been over a hundred yards in the air when Unit Alif had encountered it, and it had been at night. How much could the Cthonians have seen in those dark conditions and from that height?

Hearing Tom's questions, Rex looked around, gathering his thoughts. At his side, Hector glared at him, his eyes filled with suspicion.

Rex looked over at the airship. He glimpsed Aral standing in the doorway and realized he had a chance.

"I just came down," he finally said, his voice shaking. "Up there, they *had* sent a team down. But that's all I know. Up there," he paused and took a deep breath. He forced himself to look Tom in the eye while he pointed skyward. "They . . . the Ætherian Council . . . our governing body . . . they were after me. I escaped. Just last night. Up there, they would've killed me for sure. My only chance was to try to find you—we knew you were down here. And when I got down here, I met her," he pointed to Aral, who had stepped into the airship's open door. "She helped me."

Tom and Hector followed Rex's finger and gasped when they saw Aral.

"She's alive!" Hector exclaimed, his suspicion giving way to a mix of surprise and relief. Here was a survivor of the doomed water reconnaissance team! Surely she had answers. Surely she could fill in the gaps in the story the CCC had received about how their team of forty spotters had been killed. Tom looked back and forth between Aral and Rex, torn as to what to do next. The anger had faded from his face.

Seeing Tom's confusion, Máire spoke up, emotion straining her voice. "This is him . . . my son! This is Rex! You have to believe him. What he's saying happened to me, too! Oh, my God, I can't believe it's true, it's true . . . !" She spat her words urgently, hoping to quickly allay Tom's suspicions. She couldn't risk losing her son again. Not now. Not after everything.

The Cthonians exchanged glances, their eyes glinting as they took in this double discovery: a survivor of the failed water-seeking expedition and Máire's son.

"Can we have a few minutes?" Máire asked, looking at Tom and Hector. "Please?" Her eyes betrayed the overwhelming emotion that was bursting within her.

Tom hesitated, his fingers caressing the stock of his rifle. He glanced at the others, whose muscles seemed tensed, ready for action. He thought. He turned back to her and gaped like a fish out of water. With a relieved sigh, he slowly lowered his rifle and nodded.

"Yes. Go ahead." With that, he turned and hurried over to Aral, followed by Hector and several others.

Máire stepped back and wiped her eyes, which had filled with the stinging tears of the past. She looked at Rex and was surprised to see no expression on his face. Rather than display joy, or sadness, or regret, or even anger, he stared at her with empty eyes. His left arm hung at his side, while his right was bound tight across his chest in some sort of black sling. *How had he hurt himself?* she wondered. She imagined what he must've gone through to make it down to Cthonia under the watchful guard of the ACF and the Head Ductor. It couldn't have been easy. No matter what he'd gone through, he now stared at her as if stunned, or in shock. He kept his eyes on hers.

"Mom?" he said, his voice soft. His eyes narrowed.

"Yes?" She stepped in closer, but he took a step back.

"Mom, what are you . . . *doing* here?" He gasped as he fought back tears. As he had been searching for clues about his mother over the past week, a million thoughts had swirled through his mind—a million different scenarios of how he would react when he found her . . . *if* he found her. Now that they were together, all of his previous emotions evaporated and were replaced by an emptiness he'd never felt before. He didn't know what he felt. Despite his former, powerful emotions, all he wanted now was answers.

Máire hesitated.

"We were out of water," she said. "We had come to find some. To drill. Here. And we—I, I mean— knew Ætheria had water from the Proboscis." When she said the word "Proboscis," she looked around despondently, as if to emphasize the tragedy of its no longer being intact.

Máire turned back to Rex. He shook his head.

"No, no," he spoke with a hint of impatience in his voice. "Not why are you all here now," he tilted his head to indicate the Cthonian spotters that surrounded them. "You have to tell me, now, why *you* are here. Why did you leave home to come here? Why did you leave . . . me? Then? Before I even had a chance . . . "

Máire averted her eyes. She took a deep, slow breath.

"Franklin never told you?" Sadness and regret tinged her voice.

"Him? He never told me anything. All I ever knew was that you'd gone. That was it. For all I knew, you were still somewhere up there, but hiding. But . . . " He looked around at the barren landscape. "Why come down here?"

Máire reached out and put her hand on Rex's

unwounded shoulder. He recoiled but let her hand stay. As she spoke, he focused on the warmth of her hand, which he could surprisingly feel through his AG suit. She squeezed slightly—gently but firmly.

"I had to," her voice wavered as she spoke. "Your father—your *real* father, I mean—had his reasons, he . . . I mean, *we* couldn't stay together. We just couldn't. *I* couldn't go on. It's hard to explain. I was in trouble. I had to place you with someone else—a foster parent. I had to leave. I might've been Tossed otherwise."

Rex frowned and shook his head. "What do you mean, you *had* to leave?"

Máire hesitated, as if searching for an answer. Rex had the impression that she was trying to decide whether to lie or tell the truth. The thought that she might lie after everything sickened him.

Rex looked away and noticed Aral was surrounded by six or seven Cthonians, including Tom. She was updating them in lightning-fast speech. Rex couldn't hear every word, but he could tell she was telling them what had happened to the team that had been killed by the explosion and collapse of Tátea's Power Works. The group seemed reassured she was unharmed; but then Rex heard Tom say, "You'll of course have to process a full report when we get back." Aral's face went stony at the request. From next to the airship, she shot a knowing glance at Rex, who thought of his debriefing with Schlott. Schlott too had wanted him to fill out a report, but she'd had other intentions with his information than recording the truth of what Rex had experienced.

"Son, listen," Máire said. Rex turned back to his mother. She stepped in so that she could speak at a whisper. "Your birth father is . . . you might not believe this, but . . . " she paused and closed her eyes slowly, as if gathering the strength to continue. "Son, your father is the Head Ductor."

"What?!" Rex snapped, his mouth agape. He stepped back in shock.

"When you were born, your father didn't want

anyone to know. He didn't want anyone to know he had a . . . deformed son. Or at least, that's what he said. He was ashamed. But I wasn't."

As she spoke, Rex's face went blank. He unconsciously lifted his hand to his drooping eye and caressed the flap of skin that gave his expression a constant sad look. He shook his head slowly.

Máire continued.

"Please." She stepped forward and put both hands on Rex's shoulders. "You have to believe me when I say I fought his shortsighted, ignorant attitudes. But he'd made up his mind. That, and he'd been hoarding oxygen. For years. He was becoming paranoid. I was worried . . . about his sanity.

"When I pushed back, he gave me a choice: he would let you stay alive only if I left Ætheria and came down here, and you were given a different identity and moved into a foster home. He was going to Toss me if I refused. And his real name is Stan Leif, not Himmel."

Rex's head spun. He felt faint. His vision became

blurry, and sixteen years of pent-up emotions worked their way to the surface. He squinted hard while a painful, burning lump formed deep in his throat. He clenched his jaw to avoid crying.

"Wait, what?" he said. "My . . . *father* sent you down here? *Him*? The Head Ductor?" Rex was thunderstruck to learn that his birth father was the most powerful man in Ætheria. "But," he shook his head as if shaking off a painful thought. "Up there, they think the air down here is toxic. That's all Schlott ever talked about. So the HD . . . my father . . . he actually wanted to try to kill you?"

Máire shook her head. Anger crossed her face. "No. None of that's true. He knows the air down here is breathable. He's always known. Ever since some maintenance workers reported it years back. But apparently he didn't want to hear that. So he had them Tossed."

Rex was stunned. His faced burned with a mixture of confusion and rage. "Then why would he . . . " Rex paused, thinking of the events of the past two weeks. Of being forced into the ACF as an unprepared, underage recruit. Of his being sent down on two missions with no training. Of the mysteries of everyone in the ACF and High Command hinting that "powerful people" were watching him. He told his mother all this and asked, "What do you think was happening?"

Hearing his story, Máire's face twisted into a furious expression. She breathed deeply. She seemed to be trying to calm herself. "Knowing him, I think he was trying to control you. Maybe even get you killed. I bet he was *afraid* that you would find out the truth, and, especially as you became an adult, that you would come after him. But that didn't work . . ."

Rex shook his head and turned away—directly toward where Challies's body lay twenty yards away.

Seeing his former Protector, Rex could hold his emotions in no longer. Spitting and coughing, he swore. He cursed. He dug his left fist into the side of his head as if to push out the emotions.

But he refused to let himself seem weak in front of the others—rage overwhelmed him. He wanted revenge—revenge against the Head Ductor, his father, for causing so much pain: for separating him from his mother, for persecuting and following him, for killing Challies . . .

Yet despite his growing hatred, part of him felt deep down that he needed to confront his father. At least see him in the flesh with the knowledge of who he really was. Only then could he have closure to a life of absence.

"It's him," he finally said through clenched teeth. "Challies." He pointed at the Ætherian's body as he struggled to shake off the thoughts of what Máire had told him. "If it hadn't been for him, we'd both be . . . " Rex paused and swung around, his face red with fury. "Ahhh!" he shouted louder than he'd ever shouted in his life. His piercing scream echoed off of the rocky outcroppings. "Why?! Why is all this happening?! *Why?!*" He knelt and drove his fist into the ground again and again.

From the airship, Aral walked forward and kneeled beside Rex. She laid her hand on Rex's shoulder. And as she did, she raised her head to the sky.

What she saw made her body tense. Rex sensed the change in her and looked up through wet eyes.

"What's that?" Aral asked, pointing upward. Her voice creaked. "Way up there? Look!"

Even though the Welcans cloud was three miles up, the network of guy wires and stratoneum struts formed a network of convergent lines that allowed Rex to follow them up to the point at which they disappeared into the cloud. When he'd come down before, he hadn't paid much attention to the spectacle of the hundreds of wires and poles disappearing far above, but now he was startled by what appeared to be small specks attached to each guy wire several hundred yards below the clouds. He wiped his eyes once more and tried to make out what he was seeing.

"Everyone!" Aral shouted to the Cthonian

spotters. "Look at this!" Aral squinted upward and points. "Look at those dots, way up there. Do you see them?"

The Cthonians and Máire joined Aral and Rex out in the open and looked up. Máire kept a few yards between her and her son.

"There must be a hundred, maybe more," Hector said. "What are they?"

"They're moving," Máire added. "It looks like they're sliding down the wires." She sucked air in through her teeth. "What could it be?"

The group watched in silence as the dots descended slowly. Hector fumbled with his gear pouch around his waist and pulled out a monocular, which he raised to his eyes and focused upward. For a few seconds, he scanned the sky, trying to find what he was looking for. Then he froze, his mouth dropping open.

"Oh, my God," he said, his voice almost a whisper.

"What is it?!" Rex snapped, reaching over to the

Cthonian soldier. He was determined to make up for his fit of crying by showing the others that he could handle himself just as well as any adult. "Can I see?"

Speechless, Hector handed the monocular to Rex, who lifted it to his still stinging and watering eye and looked. At first he saw only the blurry yellow of the Welcans cloud. Following Hector's example, he reached over the top of the monocular with his middle finger and focused on several darker splotches that he'd managed to center in his field of vision. The image became clear.

When he saw what it was, he exhaled in terror. He scanned the rest of the guy wires, trying to convince himself that what he was seeing was real.

It was.

Two miles up, nearly two hundred uniformed ACF scouts were rappelling down the guy wires like a swarm of angry wasps swooping in on their target.

They were heading straight for Cthonia.

TWO

"OH, MY GOD, THEY'RE COMING FOR US!" Rex mumbled when he realized what he was seeing. He threw a panicked glance at Aral, whose pale face had gone two shades paler. Her eyes were filled with fear. Rex looked back up at the descending scouts. "But why so many?" he asked. "Something else is happening. Something's up."

"What are you talking about?" Tom said, stepping up to Rex. Máire also stepped nearer, but she kept her eyes skyward. Rex turned to Tom.

"Aral and I escaped. They were after us. We almost died. And he's the only one who helped us!"

Rex pointed at Challies's body. "And look what happened! I'm sure he was Tossed!"

Tom fumbled with his rifle. He shot a glance at the other Cthonians, who looked back and forth between Tom, Aral, Rex, and the descending legion of Ætherians. He looked around the wreckage site—at the body bags that had been lined up, the forensics kits, and Challies's body. A million different scenarios about what to do next spun in his mind. He looked back up at the descending Ætherians. He looked back at the ongoing investigation. There was clearly no time to pack up. And the Cthonians were clearly outnumbered.

His eyes suddenly cleared as he made up his mind. "Get into the airship!" he shouted. "Now! Get the engines going so that we can take off and get the hell out of here! We're coming back, but we need reinforcements!"

With jerky movements, Hector swung around toward the others. "You heard him!" he shouted, waving his arm in a circular motion. "Everyone get back into the airship we came in! Now! Let's go!"

Like horses bolting at the starting gun, the Cthonian soldiers, Aral, Máire, and Rex sprinted the fifty yards or so to the airship. Adrenaline and terror pumped through Rex's body as he ran and jumped into the massive vehicle.

He was heading to the Cthonian Cave Complex . . . with his mother.

Once inside the craft, Rex looked around. The airship's interior was identical to the one he and Aral had hid in. Only now, he didn't have time to examine the craft's details, for no sooner had they cleared the door than the soldiers began strapping themselves into seats that lined the mesh-covered walls. Three others thumped toward the front of the machine and disappeared through the hatch that Rex knew led to the cockpit. They slammed the door behind them.

"Come on!" Máire shouted to her son, pointing

to three empty seats just behind the cockpit. "Sit there!"

Máire, Aral, and Rex found their seats and began fumbling with the shoulder straps and seat belts. As the metal latches clicked, Tom and the five other Cthonian soldiers appeared through the doorway and looked around for six other empty seats, which were scattered throughout the airship's body. Tom's face was covered in sweat. He found a seat opposite Rex, sat down, and buckled himself in. Outside, the engines began to whine and roar to life, sending a high-pitched vibration shuttering through the craft.

"How far are they?" Rex shouted over the increasing noise. The metal fuselage and seats rattled as the engines gained momentum.

Tom wiped his forehead and looked at Rex.

"They're about a half mile or mile up!" he shouted, then shook his head. "We should be far away by the time they land. Don't worry!"

Rex nodded, trying to allow himself to feel some relief. Whatever relief he may have felt at escaping the ACF for a second time was replaced by the gnawing fear that this massive machine was stirring. In all his life, he'd never seen a machine this large actually work, much less fly. When Aral and he had hid in the other airship the night before, it had been turned off, asleep, harmless. Now . . .

Back on Ætheria, the only machine that even came close to being this size had been Tátea's Power Works, but even then it didn't growl, hiss, and whine like this behemoth was doing. All it had done was hum and purr as it drew up and purified water and the explosive cthoneum gas . . .

Rex's stomach lurched as the airship jolted, lifting off of the ground. He closed his eyes and breathed deeply. The movement reminded him of his first descent in the pod, when he'd come down with Yoné and Unit Alif. Then, he'd focused on his mother's face to keep him calm. Now that she was here, next to him, he did feel a certain relief that made him feel somewhat safe. But now he also had so many questions that he still wanted to ask. When would he have the chance?

With his eyes closed, Rex couldn't tell how far off the ground they were, but he could feel the airship rise and pitch as it moved. Even if his eyes had been open, he wouldn't have been able to see much through the tiny windows that ran down each side of the fuselage.

Outside, the engines' roar had grown so loud that Rex felt as though he were being shaken alive in a thundercloud. His seat rumbled and shook, and all around him the few unfastened metal buckles clanked and dinged against each other as they dangled from their straps.

"It's like this at first!" Rex heard his mother shout to his right. He felt her place her hand on his right shoulder . . . his wounded shoulder. For the first time since his injury, it didn't hurt to have someone touch it. "Just hang on!" she shouted again. "Once we get higher up, it'll get smoother!

This morning was the first time I flew in one of these as well!"

Rex nodded and opened his eyes. Tom and the Cthonian soldiers seemed relaxed. Some were readjusting their equipment straps, some were fingering their weapons. Even Aral seemed calm. *Had she ridden on one of these things before?* Not wanting to shout any more over the deafening growl of the engines, Rex decided to wait.

They continued to rise.

Pop! Swoosh!

As if the entire machine had been suspended by wires that were cut, the plane suddenly lurched downward and pitched to one side. Rex's shoulder straps and seat belt squeezed against his body, which was now being pulled by gravity to fall onto the other side of the plane. Everyone on the left side groaned against the pressure of their straps, but no sooner had the aircraft pitched to the right than it yawed to the left. Their heads banged against their headrests.

"Ahhh!" Máire shouted. "What's happening?!"

Bam!

With the force of a detonating explosion, something immense slammed into the right side of the plane, sending the machine reeling to the left. At the same time, a blinding orange-and-yellow light filled the space of every window on the right side of the fuselage.

The craft was on fire.

Beep! Beep! Beep! Beep! Beep! Beep!

A wailing alarm erupted over the din, and a red emergency light flashed above the cockpit door, bathing the passengers' faces and uniforms in red. Rex felt a surge of panic wash over him, and his eyes darted from window to window, trying to make out what was burning outside. No matter which window he looked through, all he could see was an opaque, blinding orange. He couldn't even make out any individual flames—only light.

The airship pitched forward at a steep angle, and Rex's gut heaved—they were dropping. As they fell,

Rex could now see the blazing fire licking front to back across the windows. The flames were being hurtled backward by the oncoming air of their fall.

"Brace! Brace! Brace!" What must've been the pilot's voice boomed from the same speaker as the wailing alarm. "We've lost an engine! We're going down!"

Rex's breath failed him. What did he mean, "Brace"? Seized by panic, he looked around at the others and saw that the Cthonians had each crossed their arms across their chests and leaned forward. Rex did the same. From the corners of his eyes, he saw his mother and Aral brace as well.

The plane continued to fall. How high up had they been? The rattling, roaring, clanking, and shuddering threatened to jar Rex's teeth from his head. Even the thunderstorm he'd gone through in the descent pod hadn't shaken him up this much.

And then something changed. Despite the fire outside, the pilot must've still had some control over the aircraft, for the nose lifted over the ever-increasing scream of the remaining engine. The aircraft was still falling, but it was leveling out. Rex also had the impression that its forward speed was increasing. The one remaining engine screamed and whined.

"*Here we go!*" the pilot yelled over the alarm speaker, which continued to wail. The rattling, flaming, cracking, shaking, and roaring grew even louder—so loud that Rex felt rumbling in every inch of his body. A high-pitched squeal erupted over it all, but Rex couldn't tell if the screech was coming from the engine or from one of the passengers.

Then they hit.

The screaming and roaring gave way to cracking, snapping, and ripping metal. The fuselage slid at a hundred miles per hour over the sand and rocks, which ripped at the airship, rolling it over with snapping metal and popping panes of glass. As the craft tumbled and lurched and bowled, Rex lost all sense of direction—up, down, left, or right. Everything was a blur of arms, legs, uniforms, guns, feet, hands, straps, and shouts as the passengers were tossed around with the crashing aircraft. When the windows popped, Rex felt the searing heat of the outside fire on his face. If the wings were gone, Rex couldn't tell, but at least the fuselage was holding its shape. In this, it protected the soldiers, Aral, Máire, and Rex from being crushed to death. And the pilots?

Rex had no idea how far they had slid before the airship came to a stop right-side up. Later, he would wonder if it hadn't been just seconds, though while it was happening he'd had the impression of falling and tumbling in slow motion, and, for an eternity, just waiting for one painful blow that would make everything go dark and solve all of his problems forever.

But the final blow didn't come.

"Everyone out!" Tom screamed the moment the plane stopped moving. As if muted on a radio, the earsplitting roaring, hurtling, and gashing ceased.

"Come on!" Tom screamed again as he

unbuckled his straps. "Take what you can! Your guns! Your tools! The Ætherians are still coming! We've got to get out and get cover!"

The panicked clicks and snaps of the others' unbuckling themselves filled the ravaged fuselage. As Rex freed himself, the cockpit door flew open with a crack, and all three pilots rushed out and toward the side door, which had remained closed during the crash. By the time they reached the door, everyone had unbuckled themselves and stood— including Máire and Aral. Rex glanced around and was stunned to see that, aside from a few of the soldiers whose faces were smeared with blood from gashes in their scalps, everyone had survived.

"Listen!" one of the pilots bellowed from the door. "There's fire right on the other side here. When I open, jump through and run! Don't take your time! Otherwise you'll get burned alive! You've got to get out! There's still fuel in the hold, and it could blow any second. *Go!*"

With that, he turned around and placed his

hands on the door's red release lever and pulled up and counterclockwise.

There was an earsplitting *Pop*! and a violent rush of air as the aircraft depressurized, blowing a massive gust through the opening and ripping the door from its hinges. Caught in the airstream, the first pilot flew through the door as if he'd been projected from a cannon, his arms and legs flailing about as he disappeared through a wall of flame.

"Out! Out! Out!" Tom screamed.

"Hurry!" the second pilot echoed before jumping through the fire. One by one, the Cthonian soldiers followed, weapons in hand, each vanishing through the orange curtain with a bound the moment their predecessor leapt from the burning airship.

As he waited his turn, Rex found the heat inside the fuselage becoming overwhelming, especially in his AeroGel suit, which had been designed to protect him from subfreezing temperatures, not from open flame. Underneath his clothes, his sweat flowed in torrents. At least the suit protected him from the worst of the fire's searing heat, which bit and stung his exposed face, singing his eyebrows and hair. He gritted his teeth against the pain and lifted his left arm over his face to protect himself.

Just when the pain was becoming unbearable, his turn came as the soldier in front of him leapt out. He turned around and searched among the panic-stricken faces for Aral. Just as he caught sight of her several heads back, Máire pushed him forward from behind.

"Go, son, go!" she screamed. "*Now!*"

"Okay!"

With arms and hands shaking, Rex turned back to the door. He took a deep breath, looked at the flames outside, ran, closed his eyes, and jumped.

When his feet left the metal floor, Rex was engulfed by what felt like a burst of overheated air. No sooner had he had time to register the stark change in temperature than much cooler air flooded over him. He felt no burns. He had made it through.

He opened his eyes just in time to see the ground rushing up at him. With a thud, he landed on his knees and smacked onto his wounded right shoulder, which took the full brunt of his fall, forcing the wind out of his lungs.

"Aaaaaagh!" he shrieked, reaching over with his good hand to support his shoulder. He arched his back against the sand, and for an instant felt that he would vomit from the pain of feeling his dislocated humerus grind into his still tender shoulder socket. With his breath knocked out of him, he gasped for air, gagging.

Before Rex could stand, a pair of arms wedged themselves under his armpits and lifted, pulling him away from the burning craft. He felt his heels dragging in the sand, bouncing off of small rocks. Whoever was pulling him must've been running backward. And whoever it was possessed a massive amount of strength. Every few seconds, the person would grunt in effort, but Rex could sense no change in the person's stamina.

Still fighting the intense pain in his shoulder, Rex worked his eyes open and saw that he was more than thirty yards away from the wreck. Behind him, his mom, Aral, Tom, and a dozen other Cthonian soldiers were sprinting away from the plane. Blinking against his stinging eyes and gasping for breath, Rex saw the entire group had been lucky. Both of the airship's wings had been severed, and the entire massive fuselage looked as though it had been battered by artillery that had dented but not pierced the metal. Rex then understood how their sliding had stopped.

The plane's nose had been pushed up against the first sloping rocks of the pockmarked outcropping he'd seen before. It lay at almost a right angle to the rocks, forming a giant T. Only now, the team was a mile away from the other, parked plane and the pile of rubble of Tátea's Power Works.

Regaining his composure, Rex tried to turn his head over his shoulder and look up to see where the Ætherians were, but all he saw was the sweating and straining face of the person who was dragging him across the sand. It was Hector.

As soon as he saw who had saved him, a massive wall of air slammed into the two from the direction of the aircraft, throwing a dazed Hector onto his back and causing Rex to fall once again—back-first—to the ground. No sooner had his injured body hit the Cthonian sand than a thundering, gut-wrenching detonation ripped into the two, causing Rex's hearing to ring from the earsplitting report.

Covering his head to protect himself, Rex glanced under his bent left arm to see that the aircraft had disappeared into a massive fireball that rose to the sky in a giant, billowing, flaming mushroom cloud. It had exploded. A wave of scorching heat followed, stinging his exposed head and hands.

Over the next thirty seconds, a barrage of metal fragments rained down upon the entire group, having been launched skyward. All around him, Rex heard *ziiiiip*s and *plops* and *smacks* and *cracks* and *swoosh*es as chunks of fuselage, landing gear, engine, piping, seats, cockpit, windows, ailerons, tail stabilizers, and wiring thudded into the ground, showering him with sand thrown up by the impacts. Off to his left and right, some of the soldiers screamed as debris landed on their prone bodies. And Aral? His mother? Rex heard neither of their voices. The hailstorm continued, but Rex was too afraid to lift his head to look.

As the torrent of raining wreckage subsided, Rex eased his head up and peered around. Off to his left, Máire had stood and was running toward him, worry straining her features. Rex sat up and looked himself over. He couldn't see or feel any injuries, though his entire right side throbbed from the intense pain radiating from his shoulder.

In the next instant, Máire was at his side, helping him up. Hector, who'd been dragging Rex away from the flaming airship when it had exploded, stood to his right and supported his other side. Rex noticed that Hector's face was covered with sweat.

"Rex, my sweet boy, are you okay?" she blurted, her hands rushing over his body to check for wounds. Though he could make out what she was saying, his hearing was numbed by the tinnitus from the explosion.

"I'm fine," he said, his muffled voice resonating in his skull. "Are you hurt?"

"No, I'm not, but some of the soldiers are."

Rex stepped to the side and gazed at the scene of devastation.

By now, most of the soldiers had stood and were scanning the area with their weapons drawn. At least five lay motionless on the ground. Around each, three or four Cthonians huddled, leaned over, checking for their fallen comrades' heartbeats. Even though they were spread out and dozens of yards away from him, Rex could tell just by glancing at them that they were dead—either killed from the shockwave or from falling pieces of metal.

Pacing among the carnage was Tom, who was speaking into his radio receiver. Over the ringing in his ears, Rex could make out, " . . . airship down . . . recovered one of the reconnaissance party . . . imminent advance of the Ætherians . . . armed reinforcements requested immediately." Rex assumed Tom was radioing back to the Cthonian Cave Complex.

"Rex, you're fine." Aral's voice startled him—both because he hadn't seen her approach and because his hearing was becoming clearer. He looked to his right and smiled when he saw that she, too, was unharmed.

This was the third time the two had made a narrow escape.

"What happened?" Aral asked one of the pilots, who had run up next to where they stood.

The pilot shook his head and ran his trembling hands through his sweat-drenched hair. "Catastrophic engine failure. I think some of the turbine blades disintegrated under the strain. Before we left, I was afraid something like this would happen. These airships haven't been used in years—decades, even. To take them on two missions back-to-back after so much time just sitting around . . . well, there you go. We were just lucky to have made it out." The pilot massaged his arms and lifted his head, following the thick black plume of smoke that was stretching from the burning airship to the Welcans cloud far above.

"But we're not done yet," Aral said, her voice tense.

"What is it?" Máire asked.

"Look," Aral pointed towards the east. The three others turned and looked in the direction from which they had come. About a mile away, the still smoldering pile of Tátea's Power Works interrupted the pale desert sand as a disgusting splotch of black, gray, and shreds of white. A hundred yards to the west of the debris, the Cthonian airship in which Aral and Rex had hidden rested motionless like some archaeological sculpture.

Just beyond the impact site, hundreds of ACF

troops slid down the forest of guy wires and planted their feet on the Cthonian soil.

THREE

BEFORE REX COULD REACT, TOM HAD RUSHED up behind him.

"Rex, didn't you say they were after you?" he asked with clipped breath.

"Those ACF there, I don't know . . . " Rex's voice trailed off as a mixture of fear and regret overcame him.

"What is 'ACF'?" Tom interrupted.

Rex took a deep breath and continued.

"Ætherian Cover Force. It's like a group of patrols or something. They've got weapons, too. Guns that electrocute you."

Tom jerked his head back towards his men. His eyes rested on one of the soldiers' bodies. He shook his head in disgust.

"I just called in for help," he said. "But the CCC is two days out, and the Cthonians' only remaining powered transport is *there*," he jabbed his finger in the direction of the battered airship stationed by the Power Works impact site—the one in which Aral and Rex had hidden. "And that's a mile away. Too far. Back in the CCC, all we have is eqūs and our own feet. We've got to get ready."

Tom turned around and faced the others.

"Everyone!" he shouted. "Take cover in the rocks! Over there!" He pointed toward the outcrop that had stopped the airship's sliding. The rocks stretched for two miles from west to east, like a low-altitude mountain range. They were brown and pockmarked—almost like igneous rock. But the pockmarks hadn't come from lava cooling and leaving air holes. They had come from centuries of acid rain eating away at the rock bit by bit. The crags rolled, dipped, and swirled, no doubt affording plenty of places to hide from the Ætherians. Apart from these undulations, Rex could see a constellation of small cave entrances, like dozens of mouths frozen in a yell.

Following Tom's lead, Rex broke into a run. As his feet pounded the Cthonian soil, pain wracked his body—in his wounded shoulder; in his entire right side; in his lungs that were still gasping for enough air; and on the skin of his face, which felt singed from the fiery explosion. The others ran as well, leaving five corpses lying in the open before the burning shell of the destroyed airship. Between this devastation, the acid-stripped desert, and the still-smoldering wreckage of Tátea's Power Works, Cthonia was becoming a scene from the apocalypse.

Unlike mountains with a gently sloping piedmont, the rocks burst up from the Cthonian sand, as if some massive geological forces from below had thrust them straight up. They were not vertical, but they rose at a sharp enough angle that the team had to use both arms and both legs to grip as they climbed. The pits and scars formed a natural ladder. Without too much difficulty, Rex was able to wedge his feet into hollows and crevices and push himself up, using his good left arm to steady himself from falling.

When he placed his hand on the rock, Rex was surprised at how rough and hard it was. *One fall onto this*, he imagined, *would not just break bones, but shred skin.* Foot over foot, he climbed, thrusting his left arm up every second step to the next handhold. As the more than forty Cthonians and two Ætherians climbed, their huffing, grunting, swearing, and puffing blended with the crumbling sound of pebbles and rocks being dislodged and sent tumbling below. Halfway up the bluff, the rock dipped, forming a trench fifty yards wide that the group could've hid in. But they kept going.

Rex didn't have a sense of how long they'd been climbing—maybe five, maybe ten minutes—but just as his thighs had begun to burn and tremble, he and Tom reached the crest and were able to shimmy themselves up and stand. Turning around, Rex saw he was at least twenty yards above the ground. One by one, the others joined them at the top. When Máire stood, Rex stepped over to her. Her face was covered in sweat and her hair plastered to her scalp. She was winded, and her cheeks were flushed.

"You okay?" he asked.

She nodded, but then pointed to the east. "I'm fine for now. But we're not done yet."

Rex turned and saw what she had indicated. The Ætherians were on the ground and were swarming over and around the impact site like ants. From this distance, they hardly looked human—just hundreds of black, rangy splotches crawling around. From here, Rex could hear no sounds coming from the ACF, but he imagined a scene unfolding similar to the one from that morning, when the Cthonians had arrived in their airship and began combing through the rubble. Were the Ætherians just investigating the site, or were they looking for him and

Aral? Rex liked to think that they had more important things to do, but Challies's premonitory words had left a festering pang of terror in his heart.

"Let's get down," Tom said, placing his hand on Rex's unwounded shoulder. "Come on." Rex turned around and saw that Tom and the others had their eyes glued eastward. At his order, the soldiers became unfrozen and worked their way up the bulbous and waving rocks.

Up ahead, Rex noticed the rocks seemed to form a long, low wall—one that could hide the entire group. Tom must've seen it as well, because in one bound he leapt onto and behind it. As Rex prepared to do the same, he glanced to his right and froze.

"Tom, did you see that?" he said, pointing.

Tom turned around, his body and legs now hidden by the wall.

"What is it?"

"There. The rocks slope up here, like a walkway. We could've just walked up." Rex *humph*ed in frustration at their wasted effort. Gripping the wall with his left hand, he shimmied his right leg up and over, and, like someone getting onto a horse for the first time, he worked his body up into a straddling position before letting himself drop down below.

Rex settled into position. Around him, a chorus of crunches and cracks echoed as the others planted their feet onto the brittle rock and crouched, pulling their heads from view. Máire slid into place to Rex's left, and Aral was next in line.

To his right, Tom leaned his back against the rock wall and ran his hands through his drenched hair. He clenched his jaw and stared straight ahead. He opened his mouth to speak, but as he did, he looked at no one—just the expanse of surging rocks stretching out before him.

"I've only ever known one Ætherian—well, two now," he said in a whisper. Rex noticed that Tom's voice was going hoarse. "I don't know how they think, much less what those ACF—or whatever you call them—have as their goal." He paused, thinking. "But I can tell you," he turned and faced Rex, "if *I* were with them, and if *I* were on a reconnaissance or even capture mission, I would come and investigate this burning wreck. Because right now, that's the only show happening in this godforsaken desert."

At Tom's words, Rex turned and eyed the black smoke that billowed upward from the still burning crash site. The plume was at least thirty yards wide at its base, but it had already stretched up to over a mile high, where it had expanded, tornado-like, into a damning beacon hundreds of yards wide. There was no way the Ætherians wouldn't see it. What Rex didn't know—and couldn't predict—was whether they would come investigate.

FOUR

A S THEY WAITED BEHIND THE WALL OF ROCK, Rex's mind raced. He could think of only two reasons why the ACF would've come down.

First, to pick up where the decimated Unit Alif had left off. When Rex had gone down with Yoné and the others, their job had been to scout out the site and come back with information. Now Deputy Head Schlott, the Ætherian Council, and no doubt the Head Ductor himself were convinced the Cthonians were hostile. They'd thought that even before the Power Works had been attacked. Losing a team of ACF to enemy fire could only confirm that suspicion. *What is their plan? To attack the Cthonians? Surely not,* he thought. Based on what Rex had told Schlott—and written in his official report—the Ætherian Council had to know the Cthonians' firepower was superior to the Ætherians' puny Stær guns. If the two sides fought, there would be a slaughter. Unless, of course, the Ætherians could overwhelm these forty-odd Cthonians with their numbers?

Second, Rex wondered if the ACF had come down in search of him and Aral. That seemed possible, especially given how the two were being chased back on Ætheria after their escape. But would the Ætherian Council send down *that* many ACF? When Rex had seen them sliding down the wires, he had the impression there was an ACF scout on every guy wire supporting the Ætherian archipelago. That had to be hundreds. Would they send down that many scouts just to find him?

Was he *that* important?

Rex shook his head. He couldn't believe they'd

come down just for him. What worried him was the comparison between the Cthonians' numbers and the Ætherians' numbers. Several hundred to forty.

To Rex's right, Tom shifted position, causing a few pebbles to slip and crumble underfoot. He inched his head up from behind the wall and peered down toward the desert below. Rex watched Tom's eyes dart about, until they settled on something off to Tom's left.

"What do you see?" Rex whispered.

"See for yourself. They're still far away."

Rex turned and eased his head up. When his face cleared the top of the wall, a gentle breeze greeted him, cooling his scorched features. He blinked against the wind and directed his gaze to where Tom had been looking: down the outcropping and to the left.

There, about five hundred yards away, Rex saw that Tom's hunch had been right. What looked to be about thirty ACF were working their way across the sand in the direction of the burning plane.

They had spread out in an angle formation, with one scout at the front. *Who is that?* Rex wondered about the lead scout, his mind scanning the ACF Protectors of higher rank that he'd met or seen. They were still too far away for Rex to discern any details, but he could see two vital details: their arms were extended in front of them, gripping something. This had to be a Stær gun—so they were ready for a fight. Second, they were all wearing their SCRMs—the Self-Contained Respirator Masks that Rex wore when he came down to Cthonia for the first time. Rex lifted his eyes to the Power Works wreckage and the parked airship beyond. The dark forms of the remaining ACF were swarming around the site.

A thought struck.

Rex slid back into a sitting position and leaned over to Máire.

"Mom?" he whispered.

"Yes?"

"I wonder . . . "

"What is it?"

"When I came down before, I saw I could breathe here. So did the others. But they were killed. I tried to tell Schlott, but she didn't believe me."

"I'm not surprised. Remember? The Head Ductor knows the air is fine down here. But he doesn't want anyone else in Ætheria to know. If they did . . . " she trailed off, her eyes going glassy.

"Then what?"

"If everyone in Ætheria knew you could breathe down here, they'd probably all come down. He'd be out of power, then." She looked around. "It's just now that water's become the issue . . . "

"Right. So if we can get them to take their masks off, they would see, right? That must be the entire ACF down there. If all of them knew they could breathe, do you think . . . ?"

Máire turned and stared at her son with incredulous eyes. "How?"

Rex scrunched up his face. "I don't know. What if I talked to them?"

"What?" Máire's voice became alarmed. "They would capture you right away! You're a fugitive! Like me!"

Rex fell silent. He looked over at the Cthonian spotters, his eyes scanning their weapons. Seeing them made him think about his own botched experience with his Stær gun, when he'd dropped it in the mud and that was all it had taken for the gun to malfunction. But here . . . he'd seen the Cthonians fire their weapons from the airship. Never in his life had he imagined such a thing as possible—roaring cannons that shredded his teammates from a half mile away. Whereas those Stær guns . . . all they could hope to do was temporarily paralyze someone, and then, only if they were within fifty yards or so.

Then he remembered that Tom had called in reinforcements from the Cthonian Cave Complex. They'd be here in a day or two. What would happen to them—the Cthonians, Máire, Aral, and

Rex—during that time? Could they remain hidden until help arrived? What would they do for water? If the Ætherians were still there when the Cthonians came, then what? Because Rex knew the Ætherians felt threatened, he could only imagine a war breaking out right in front of them—one in which the Ætherians would be outgunned. Yes, Rex had been pursued by the ACF, but the Ætherians were his people—his friends, his classmates, and even the few members of the ACF he'd gotten to know over the past week and a half.

Thirty minutes passed. No one spoke. Rex's thoughts surged.

He turned again and looked over the outcropping. He gave a start at what he saw: the ACF had advanced on the burning airship much faster than he had expected. All he had to do was shout and they would hear him.

As his mind prepared him for what he had decided to do, he felt his heart thump faster and stronger. His lungs had recovered from his earlier fall, but he soon found his breath coming in shorter gasps. His hands became clammy, and his legs began to tremble.

He turned to Tom.

"Tom, I think I can talk to them," he whispered.

Tom snapped his head at Rex, fury distorting his features. "What?! Are you crazy? What do you think's going to happen?! Why would you take a risk like that?"

"Rex, son, no . . . " Máire implored behind him. She placed her hand on his healthy shoulder and pulled. He yanked his shoulder from her grip.

"Tom," Rex continued, "your weapons are better than theirs. Theirs can only shoot a little distance and just electric shocks . . . but they won't kill you. I have something to confess: I was in that group your airship shot at a few days ago. I saw what your guns can do."

Tom's face burned red at Rex's revelation. He reached for his radio transmitter, but hesitated as Rex continued to speak.

"But it was a mistake," Rex said. "Then. Our team was riding out to *talk*—to tell you that we knew everything was a mistake. The Ætherians had it wrong. The Cthonians had it wrong to think we'd killed your people. Aral told me that. We wanted to reach you to talk. But then my, my Point, then . . . *her* Stær gun accidentally went off and the airship fired," he lied. "We *never* shot back. Didn't you see that? We just ran. Aral and I were the only ones to make it back up alive. Everyone else was killed . . . " Rex's voice trailed off.

Tom never took his eyes off of Rex. His hand hovered over his radio receiver. In his heart, he felt he believed what he was being told, but his duty to report this to the CCC fueled a painful internal debate. They would want an investigation . . . interrogations . . . corroborations of his story . . . But now, now they were stuck between a rock and a hard place. An armed and hostile faction was approaching, and this boy was offering to try and talk to them. Tom's mind weighed the outcomes. In one thing, Rex was right: the Cthonians had superior weapons. More than that, they had the drop on the Ætherians. From their protected position high above, these forty-odd Cthonians would easily defeat the thirty-some Ætherians. And the other hundreds over at the Power Works wreckage site? What would happen if fighting broke out and they came for backup?

Tom didn't have long to make up his mind. He peeked up once more to glance at the ACF, but jerked his head back. But this time, the Point scout's eyes happened to be trained on the crest of the outcropping, where he thought he'd seen some movement. There was no doubt in his mind that he'd seen someone looking at them.

"You there!" the ACF scout shouted. "Up there! Rex?! Rex Himmel, is that you?!"

Even though the scout's voice was muffled by the rubber of the SCRM, Rex recognized the voice. It was Roman, the Protector who'd been assigned to guard him in the Sanatorium. The one whom

Challies had dazed to help Rex escape. Hearing his name now, Rex wondered if Schlott had not made Roman responsible for tracking down Rex. Why the hundreds of other ACF?

Without another word or glance to Tom, Máire, or Aral, Rex stood, his left hand in the air. Máire stifled a scream and snatched at her son's legs.

"Yes! I'm here!" Rex shouted, his voice echoing over the cave-filled rocks. The group of ACF swung their arms in his direction, their bodies tense. Rex knew they were pointing their Stær guns at him, but he also knew he was out of range.

Without acknowledging Tom, Máire, Aral, and the others, who were shushing him and grabbing at his legs for him to get down, Rex shimmied back over the wall and walked to the incline he'd seen earlier. Before he started down, he cast a glance backward, but the others remained hidden.

"Keep an eye out for me," he hissed just loud enough for them to hear. There was no reply. As Rex headed down toward the Ætherians, he couldn't shake the fear that Tom hadn't heard him. Surely they would keep watch and cover him if anything went wrong? Surely they wouldn't leave him on his own? With these thoughts, Rex began to doubt his decision.

Rex lifted his eyes to the ACF, who kept their darkened SCRM goggles and their Stær guns trained on him. At this point, the rock was even enough that Rex didn't have to watch every footfall. As he walked, he cast a glance to the rock face on his left, which was interrupted by three dark, gaping cave entrances. When he passed one, Rex glanced in but could make out nothing beyond just a few feet. After that, there was only dark. He wondered how deep the caves were, or if they formed an underground network.

With heart pounding, Rex reached the Cthonian sand. Here he paused and lifted his hands, so that Roman and the other ACF could see that he had no weapons. With Roman's face covered by the SCRM, Rex couldn't make out his features. He wondered what emotions might be going through Roman right then. After all, it had been his job to guard Rex in the hospital, and while on duty Roman had been stunned from behind by Challies, one of his own teammates, allowing Rex and Aral to escape. Was he angry? Did he feel betrayed? Or was he afraid of the Head Ductor's wrath?

Rex approached his former guard. As he neared, part of him expected to be stunned by Roman's or one of the others' Stær guns. But then the thought hit: in Ætheria, all criminals were supposed to be tried before . . . punishment. No, the Stær gun blasts weren't lethal, but perhaps Roman had other instructions?

"Roman?" Rex asked when he got to within three yards. He stopped as he spoke, but never lowered his hands.

"Rex? We have to take you. Now." Roman's voice sounded closed-in and rubbery behind the mask.

Rex didn't answer. He scanned the line of ACF

scouts that faced him, trying to recognize some-one—anyone—by their body shape and posture. Recognizing no one, he stood on his toes to look beyond the team at the Power Works impact site. From here, and this close to the ground, he could only just make out the airship and a few wisps of smoke rising from the rubble. He couldn't see any of the ACF scouts.

"Why are so many of you down here?" Rex asked.

The question caught Roman by surprise. His head jerked back. "To secure the area and to look for water and . . . supplies. You knew we were planning that."

"No, I didn't."

"*And* we were looking for you and that Cthonian, of course. Where is she?"

"Roman, does anything seem strange about me?"

"What?"

"I'm not wearing a mask." To emphasize his point, Rex took in several deep breaths. "Do you know why? It's because you can breathe here. It's not like they said."

"What are you talking about?!" The tone in Roman's voice betrayed his confusion, as if he'd imagined this scene playing out much differently than it was. He'd expected a fight or at least some resistance, but now all he was getting was riddles. His patience drew thin.

———

"What's happening?" Máire hissed at Tom, who'd raised his eyes above the rock wall and was looking down at what was unfolding below.

He shook his head, dumbfounded. "I don't know. Rex and that Ætherian are talking."

"Can you hear what they are saying?"

Tom shook his head.

From Tom's vantage point, the scene reminded him more of a military commander giving quiet orders to a platoon of soldiers. Only here, the commander was Rex. None of the Ætherians seemed alarmed, but they never lowered their Stær guns. The Ætherian lead man also still had his weapon raised, but his arms were bent. Was he lowering his gun?

What is he doing? Tom thought, scrunching up his eyes in disbelief. Whatever Rex and the lead were saying to each other, Rex's arms began to wave about. He became animated and was raising his voice. Some of his words made their way up to Tom, " . . . air . . . survive . . . you can breathe!"

Rex's agitation had an effect on the Ætherians, who—even from this distance—visibly became nervous. They began shifting their weight from leg to leg and gripping their weapons tighter. The lead Ætherian also shook his head and took a step toward Rex.

Something was about to happen.

"Pssst!" Tom hissed to his soldiers, whose eyes were already on him. He jabbed his finger toward where Rex was standing and lifted his rifle, shaking it once to tell the others to get ready.

With the hushed noise of rocks and pebbles crunching underfoot, the forty-odd soldiers eased up onto their haunches and laid their rifles across the top of the wall. Tom motioned to Máire and Aral to keep their heads down. Máire shot him a pathetic look with her eyes, one that said, "Help him." Tom nodded and aimed his rifle. Looking down the sights, he trained his barrel on the lead Ætherian. He steadied his breath so that his rifle would remain steady. The Cthonian soldiers now looked like a squadron waiting in ambush.

Tom didn't expect the first move to come from Rex. In the middle of what seemed to be a heated argument, Rex lunged at the lead Ætherian's head with his outstretched left arm and snatched at the Ætherian's mask.

The Ætherian hardly had time to react. The lead man dropped his pistol and lifted his hands to clutch at his mask. It was too late. Rex had a firm hold of the supply tube protruding from the mouth and nose area. The two tussled in place like wrestlers trying to trip each other.

In the next instant, three of the Ætherians had swarmed around Rex. Holstering their pistols, they latched onto his shoulders and arm and heaved him several yards backward into the sand. He landed on his back and did a backward somersault, his legs flopping up and over his head. The three who had pulled him off stepped back and shouted to the others. The moment they were out of the way, two other ACF raised their pistols and fired. Bursts of sparks erupted from their weapons as glowing charges flew out towards Rex, who was scrambling to get to his feet.

He never made it. Arching his back as one hundred thousand volts coursed through him, Rex slumped to the ground, his body writhing and twitching.

Next to him in the sand, the Ætherian's mask lay, its supply tube ripped in half from the force of the three ACF yanking him away from their lead man.

In the same moment that the Stær guns hurled their charges at Rex, Tom and the Cthonian soldiers opened fire.

With ear-shattering reports, their first bullets tore through the bodies of the two ACF who had shot Rex. Like marionettes whose strings had been cut, the two men dropped to the sand, lifeless. As their Stær guns fell, the electric charges stopped coursing and Rex's body ceased to thrash about. He now lay just as still as the two dead ACF scouts.

Behind them, Roman, now without his SCRM, grasped at his nose and mouth and ran toward the burning plane, his path jerking left and right. Stricken by panic, the other Ætherians scattered, but not before a few aimed toward the bluff and fired their Stær guns in the Cthonians' direction. Based on what Rex had told him, Tom had assumed they were out of range of the Ætherians' weapons, but the charges reached all the way to the rock wall, bouncing off with popping *clinks* and causing Tom's and the others' skin to tingle and their hair to bristle. Their radio receivers cracked and popped, hissing as their circuitry was disabled by the surge of electricity. The ACF clearly had weapons more powerful than what Rex had reckoned.

The Cthonians continued their assault as the Ætherians fled toward the airship, which was now the only cover available. More than that, it abutted the outcropping, giving the Ætherians access to the cave-ridden rocks.

Behind the rock wall, Aral and Máire covered their ears and tucked their heads down as the rifles exploded in fury above them. Down below, massive divots of sand erupted ten feet in the air where the bullets missed their targets; but when they hit, the Ætherians tumbled to the ground—some lifeless, some twisting in agony. Before they made it to cover behind the airship, five ACF fell, their bodies joining the five Cthonians who had been killed by falling debris from the plane's explosion.

One of the dead was Roman.

Rex's plan had failed.

FIVE

"COME ON!" TOM SHOUTED TO HIS SOLDIERS. He stopped firing and stood, gauging the scene. The last of the Ætherians had disappeared behind the flames. Tom pointed to one of the soldiers and swept his arm over half of the group. "You twenty, sweep up and over the rocks to keep them from coming up and hiding in the caves. Make sure your radio is turned to channel two in case I need you. You others, come with me down there after them! And you two, get Rex and bring him up! We've got to get him before the other Ætherians get here!"

Tom cast a worried glance in the direction of the still intact airship and the impact site of Tátea's Power Works. He was certain the other Ætherians had heard the gunfire and would be coming to their comrades' aid. At a mile away, that gave the Cthonians maybe fifteen minutes before a new attack would begin. He looked around at the rocks. Their only chance would be to take cover in the caves and try to hold off the Ætherians until . . .

He unhooked his radio receiver from his belt and clicked transmit. The radio made no sound. Tom looked at it and saw that the red power light was off. He clicked the handset off and on several times, but got no reaction.

"Does anyone's radio work?" he shouted to the others. The Cthonians reached to their belts and toyed with their receivers, but all of the team's electronics had been overwhelmed by the jolt from the Stær guns. A chorus of "No," "Doesn't work," and "Dead!" caused Tom to swear and spit.

"We're on our own!" he said, attaching his radio

back to his belt and jumping over the rock wall. The others followed, their rifles sweeping back and forth in front of them. They ran down the incline to the sandy flat of the desert. Hector and his soldiers scrambled in the other direction, heading west over the rocks.

"You two!" Tom shouted to Máire and Aral, the only two unarmed persons in the group. "Come down to these caves here," he pointed down and to the left at the caves that lined the path. "I'll bring him over. We've got to get cover."

Máire and Aral bounded over the rock wall and surveyed the scene. Máire's face was twisted with worry and anguish.

"What happened?" she asked, her voice trembling.

"Rex snatched off one of their masks, and they shot him with one of those electric things." Tom turned to follow his soldiers.

"Oh, my God! Rex!" Her thoughts swam back sixteen years to what she could remember about the Stær guns. In her mind, she knew they weren't lethal; but in her heart she felt her son was in mortal danger. She shot a terrified look down to where Rex lay. From this distance, she couldn't tell if he was moving. Her eyes settled on the SCRM that lay in a heap beside her son's body.

Her expression lightened as a thought struck.

"Wait!" she shouted. Tom paused and turned to her as his soldiers stormed down the incline.

"What is it?" he snapped, irate.

"Get them to take off their masks," she said.

"What?!"

"The other Ætherians are going to be coming. And our help is a day out. We *can't* hold that long. Show them they can breathe here. Show them! Maybe they'll realize too when they see you're not wearing any masks. They're being forced to live way up there in impossible conditions. That's why I left! Show them! It's our only way!"

Tom hesitated, his face flushed from the adrenaline of combat. He looked eastward, in the direction of the remaining hundreds of Ætherians. He looked back at the flaming airship just fifty yards away—by now, all of the Ætherians had disappeared behind it. He looked at Rex, who was being lifted from the sand by two of his soldiers. He looked at the rest of his soldiers, who had already begun to work their way toward the tail of the airship. Only five seconds passed between Máire's plea and his reply, but in that time a million contradictory thoughts stormed through his mind.

"Just get in the cave!" he snapped. "They're bringing him over. I'll take care of this!"

With that, he bounded down the hill, sprinting to catch up with his soldiers. By now, the two who were carrying Rex were just yards away. Keeping her eyes on her son, Máire worked her way down, followed by Aral. One of the soldiers carrying Rex looked up and saw her.

"There!" he shouted, nodding at one of the caves with his head. On the left side of the path, three cave entrances opened up. When they'd climbed up the steeper rock face before, Máire hadn't seen these, because they'd been hidden in the folds and waves of the crag. The soldier had nodded to the middle one.

When Máire reached the cave mouth, she understood why. Compared to the first cave she walked by, this one was much deeper, its passage winding and disappearing into the dark. There, she and Aral paused, waiting for the two soldiers to reach them before entering.

As if sensing Máire's thoughts, the first soldier tried to force a smile and said amid huffs, "He's alright. Just knocked out. He's breathing fine, and everything else looks okay. No other injuries."

Máire felt a flood of relief and gazed at Rex's face as the two soldiers carried him into the cave. He looked asleep. Despite her fears, she couldn't help but feel proud of him at that moment—not just because of his courage in pulling off the Ætherian's mask, but in everything that he must've done up until now to find her. His shoulder was already injured, but how? Had he gotten hurt along the way? What kind of risks had he taken? He'd said that he'd escaped, but how? She hoped that this fighting would soon end so that she and Rex could start over and make up for the sixteen years she felt that she'd lost in fleeing from the Head Ductor of Ætheria.

Máire and Aral followed the two soldiers into the cave. Even though there was no direct sunlight on Cthonia, she felt the temperature drop by a few degrees. As she stepped into the dark, her eyes soon adjusted. She saw that they had entered a cavern that stretched down and quite far. From her position near the entrance, she couldn't see where it ended.

The soldiers walked another thirty feet or so and laid Rex on the cool rock. Máire knelt by her son while Aral remained standing. From here, the incline back to the entrance was steep enough that they couldn't see outside—only diffuse light trickled back down to them.

"Listen," one of the soldiers said, "you three stay here. You're hidden. We'll come back for you. If you hear fighting outside, don't come out."

Images of a swarming army of ACF flashed through Máire's mind—she saw them teeming over the desert and the rocks like angry insects, exploring every nook for prey. Would they think to explore the rocks? Or would they stay in the open desert? She knew that few ACF had ever laid eyes on Cthonia before, and these were limited to those whose job it was to descend the guy wires or in the descent pods to maintain Ætheria's support structure. From what she could remember, she knew the ACF never had any reason to go exploring down here. Not only because their mission had only ever been maintenance, but the Head Ductor had made sure that everyone in Ætheria believed that Cthonia was nothing but an inhospitable wasteland—one whose toxic air would kill you within seconds.

Aral must've been thinking the same thing.

Just as Máire's fears were gaining momentum, the Cthonian spoke up.

"What if they come looking in the caves?" she asked.

The soldier's answer revealed irritation.

"What do you want me to say?" he said. "This has never happened before. All we can do now is hope." With that, he and his partner turned and left.

SIX

BACK DOWN BELOW, TOM CAUGHT UP WITH his soldiers, who advanced on the broken airship. The fire had abated. The blackened, wingless machine had become little more than a hulking metal tube with flames and smoke lapping out of the door and shattered windows. The front was jammed against the rocky outcropping, almost as if it had been rammed on purpose into the crags.

In a radius of a hundred yards all around the wreck, fragments of the plane littered the ground. As they approached, the Cthonians could still feel the heat radiating from the fire, though its intensity had become bearable—unlike when the airship had first exploded. Step by step, they advanced with their weapons pointed forward. They knew that behind the wreckage, nearly thirty armed Ætherians were waiting for them. But where? Had they used the cover of the plane to run farther away? Or were they huddled there with their Stær guns drawn, hoping to mount a defense against the Cthonians? Given how they'd fled, Tom was sure the Ætherians were more afraid of them than the Cthonians were of the Ætherians. The Cthonians had a psychological and a military advantage.

The soldiers reached the bodies. In all, there were ten: five Cthonians and five Ætherians. Tom scanned the scene. He knew all of the Cthonians were dead from the impact of the falling debris. He wasn't sure about the Ætherians.

"Check them!" he shouted, his eyes darting from Ætherian to Ætherian. At least two were squirming in the sand, one within a few yards of where Tom walked. When he shouted, the Ætherians jerked their heads in his direction and began attempting to crawl away on their backs, pulling themselves backward on their elbows. Tom saw that the closest person's hands were empty. He scanned around for the weapon, but saw none. The person was unarmed.

This close, he could see the Ætherians were dressed like Rex: each wore a skintight outfit covering them from head to toe. Unlike Rex, each wore what looked like some sort of utility belt with small pouches girdling their waist. Each also wore one of those ridiculous-looking face masks, connected via a floppy rubber tube to a foot-long canister strapped to their backs. Seeing these masks up close, Tom thought of Máire's words. Doubt filled his mind, but mixed with the doubt was a suspicion that she was onto something. He stepped up to the wounded Ætherian and looked down.

With the Ætherian's face covered, Tom couldn't tell if he was looking at a man or a woman. Whoever it was, they had a neat bullet hole midway up their right thigh. The entire top of the leg was covered in blood, which had stained the sand underneath and was leaving a crimson trail as the person inched away. Tom hesitated. Exhausted from the effort and the loss of blood, the Ætherian collapsed onto their back, their chest heaving from exertion.

Tom shook his head as he made up his mind. He looked up and shouted to the others.

"If any are alive, pull off their masks!"

The others nodded and continued toward the plane. As for Tom, he stepped up to the wounded Ætherian. And, keeping his rifle pointed at the Ætherian's chest, he reached over and clamped his fist around the rubber supply tube, just as he'd seen Rex do moments before.

At his touch, the Ætherian emitted a muffled scream from within the mask and struck out at Tom with both hands. It was a man. As his fists struck Tom's arms and shoulders, Tom could feel the man had little force left. The blows felt more like irritating slaps than punches meant to do harm.

"Relax!" Tom barked. "I'm not going to harm you!"

With that, he jerked at the supply tube. In a final attempt to protect himself from asphyxiation, the Ætherian clutched at his mask. Tom was stronger. With a soft *whoosh* as the suction was released, he wrenched the mask from the Ætherian's face and tossed it aside with a *plop*.

In all his years as a Cthonian soldier, Tom had never seen an expression of more abject terror than he did when he unmasked the Ætherian. The man's eyes bugged from his head, and, despite the Ætherians' natural dark complexion compared to Cthonians', all of the color left his face. He squealed and flailed at the sand, looking for his mask. Tom kicked it away and stood up. The man screamed again, this time with much less force. He hadn't taken a breath since his mask came off. Tom took a step back.

"Calm down," he said, "you can breathe here. Look," Tom took in a few deep breaths of air to show the Ætherian. "It's not like we're living in some vertical world above the clouds here."

Just as the Ætherian's eyes began to roll back into his head from lack of oxygen, his lungs betrayed him and drew in a massive gulp of air. Almost instantly, his eyes regained focus and the color returned to his face. His flailing limbs relaxed, and Tom even had the impression that the Ætherian's chest was growing in capacity with each breath.

The man looked back at Tom with soft eyes. "What the . . . ?" he muttered, unable to complete his sentence. He took a few more deep breaths as if to convince himself, and then settled back into the sand, his eyes skyward. "I can't . . . it's not . . . we . . . you . . . "

"I told you." Tom smirked. He rejoined the others heading toward the tail of the airship. Máire's idea was the best they had.

SEVEN

BACK IN THE CAVE, REX WAS STIRRING.
Máire knelt next to her son while Aral paced.

"This is the second time in a day he's been hit with electricity," the Cthonian said.

Máire gave a start. "What? When? What happened?"

"Yesterday. We were coming down with the descent pods. He was hit by lightning. He was knocked out when I opened up his pod."

"What? Lightning?"

"He needs a rest, I think. He was complaining

about headaches earlier, when we were hiding. But he got some food and water."

On the cool rock floor, Rex groaned and scrunched up his face. His left fingers twitched. Máire turned to her son, reached out, and placed her hand on his forehead. She was relieved to feel that his skin felt normal: sweaty, yes, but not clammy or sick. The thought that he'd been electrocuted twice in a day made her nauseous. How many shocks like that could anyone take? And just a sixteen-year-old?

As her worries took root, she realized: this was her son. Her Rex, who she'd thought she would never see again. Earlier, when he'd rushed from the plane, both mother and son had been too overwhelmed by contradictory emotions to realize how powerful the moment was. When she'd last laid eyes on Rex in Ætheria, he'd been a newborn. His face had been round with a double chin, and the baby fat on his arms and legs had made creases in his forearms and thighs. Now here he was, almost an adult. In the two weeks of his life she'd been present, she remembered worrying about the damage his irregular birth had caused to his face and brain. During labor, the doctors had had to anesthetize Máire because they'd realized that, once into the birth canal, Rex's umbilical cord was choking him to death. They had to act fast. As soon as she was unconscious, they'd completed the delivery by C-section. They'd saved his life, but the damage had been done. Half of his face had been paralyzed, and the doctors had worried about brain damage. During the days after his birth, Máire had watched her son nonstop for signs of anything that seemed strange, abnormal. Aside from his drooping face, she'd seen nothing.

She never got to see him grow and develop. Rex's father, Head Ductor of Ætheria, demanded that no one know the boy was his. He was ashamed of Rex's deformity. He thought that if the Ætherians knew he'd produced a weak heir, they would see him as weak. They would question him. They would challenge him. They would threaten him. Máire had objected at his blind paranoia, but one night, while mother and baby slept, he transferred the newborn to a foster father. When she'd awoken the following morning, Máire had been hysterical. In her fury, she threatened to reveal to others in Ætheria the secret that the HD had kept so close for so long: that the air on Cthonia was breathable. How he'd discovered this, she'd never known, but in one night of drunken passion, he'd revealed the secret to her before swearing her to secrecy. They'd loved each other then. But over the years, he'd become more and more suspicious and stingy with the bottled oxygen in Ætheria. He'd always said that it was for the people's own good, but Máire knew better. She knew all he wanted was to stay in power in his fantasy vertical world—oxygen or not. With her son gone, she threatened to reveal everything. The HD had at first tried to calm her by telling her the name of the boy's foster father, but she only threatened to find him and take her son back.

"Do it, and I'll have you Tossed!" he'd sworn at her threat, his face blue with rage. It was then that she knew she had to flee. She knew about the Cthonians, though at the time all she knew was what everyone in Ætheria knew: that they were a stubborn tribe of land-dwellers who hid out in caves and ate and drank God-knows-what in the inhospitable world of Cthonia. Despite not knowing what lay below the Welcans cloud, she knew what fate awaited her above.

So one night when the HD was at work late, she wrote a note to Franklin Strapp, her son's foster father, and sent it via one of the ACF guards in the HD's complex. With that, she entered the subterranean Larder on Island Twelve, put on one of the service harnesses, and plunged into the unknown. She never found out if Franklin had received her note.

"Mom?" Rex managed to say, his eyes still closed. Máire leaned over him and stroked his hair with her hand.

"I'm here."

"He's been looking for you," Aral whispered

behind her. Máire turned and looked at the Cthonian. "I've heard so much about him from you and others—about his name and face, I mean—that I recognized him when he came down before. Ever since then, all he's talked about is finding you. I think that's all he wanted."

A warmth spread through Máire's torso and limbs. It was a warmth she hadn't felt in sixteen years. It was the warmth of a mother's unconditional love, combined with the relief of getting her lost son back safely.

"Mom?" Rex said again. He opened his eyes and looked at her.

"I'm here, baby."

"I'm not a baby."

Máire smiled. "Of course you're not. Look at you. Look what you've done. I'm so proud."

"Proud?" Rex worked his legs and left arm. Pins and needles shot up and down his body as his system awoke from the electrical stun.

"Yes, I'm proud."

"But . . . what do you know?"

"I know you're here, and that's all that really matters. Can you tell me how?"

Rex sat up and rubbed his head. He winced at the pain in his temples. His head throbbed, but he forced himself to tell Máire his story: from being recruited into the ACF, to the attack, to coming down to inspect the wreckage, to meeting Aral, to helping her escape, and to their final descent the day before. As he spoke, tears welled up in Máire's eyes, and she shook her head in disbelief.

"Mom, Dad's dead."

"What?" she started, thinking about the Head Ductor. As Rex continued, she realized he was talking about Franklin Strapp—the person responsible for bringing Rex up from a baby.

"He was working. In the Power Works, when it was attacked. He must've fallen over the edge when the building fell." Rex spoke with no emotion in his voice, as if he were reciting lines in a play for the first time.

"I know," Máire said. "Or I thought as much. I found his Tracker back there in the rubble. But I'm here, now, and I'm not leaving you again."

"Mom . . . " Rex mumbled, his throat squeezing as tears welled up. "I found your letter and picture in Dad's things. Mom . . . I missed you so much."

Before he could finish his sentence, Máire leaned forward and embraced her son. He buried his head in the crook of her neck and wept, his body wracked with sobs. Máire felt his warmth, even through his insulated AeroGel suit. In an instant, the memory of holding her baby boy came hurtling back. It was as if she could recognize her son by touch alone, and now she never wanted to let him go. She rocked him back and forth like a small child, humming a lullaby in his ear. Hearing her soothing voice, Rex sobbed even harder. He felt as though he'd heard this voice before, and he knew that he had: sixteen years ago when he was several days old. He hadn't heard it since.

For the first time in his life, he felt part of a family.

"Mom?" Rex said into Máire's neck. He pulled back, leaving a wet spot of tears on her shoulder and the top of her collar.

"What is it?"

"What are we going to do? About this?" He nodded back toward the cave's entrance. "About the Head Ductor? About the people back home?"

Máire sat up straight and let out a deep sigh. "I don't know, son. I don't know. I've spent the last sixteen years of my life thinking about that, believe me." She shot a worried glance toward the light. "Right now our main job is to get out of this mess. For that we can only wait on Tom and the others."

She cocked her head toward the cave entrance and looked up at Aral. "I haven't heard anything since we came in. Have you?"

Aral shook her head.

"What happened after they shot me?" Rex asked. He then looked around and asked, "How long have we been here?"

"Maybe thirty minutes?" Máire said. "There was a

firefight. Several of the Ætherians were killed. They hid behind the plane. The Cthonians were heading there when we came here."

"Dead?" Rex muttered, his eyes wide. "And Roman? His mask? Did I get it off?"

Máire nodded. "That's when they shot you."

"Shh," Aral said, interrupting the two. "Be quiet for a second and let me listen."

Máire and Rex tried to soften and slow their breathing, which had calmed since their upsurge of emotion. Hearing that a deadly battle had just occurred because of his trying to convince Roman that he could breathe on Cthonia, Rex felt his nerves go tight and an unpleasant sense of unease fill his chest. Still, he tried to listen.

As the three silenced their rustling, they became aware of a strange, echoing quality of the sound in the cave—as if they were in a giant tube. The hollow noise reminded Rex of his descent into the Proboscis before its destruction. There, the slightest movement had become amplified and distorted. If you closed your eyes here, it would be difficult to orient yourself, because the resonating would throw off all sense of direction.

No sign of life came from outside. No gunfire, no voices, no movement. Rex wondered what could be happening. Was Tom okay? The others? As he listened, he imagined a stealthy, silent group of ACF scouts working their way up the rocky incline and to the mouth of their cave, Stær guns drawn. The cave was deep, but if a group of Ætherians rushed in now, the three would be caught in a trap.

Rex rotated his head to the back of the cave and squinted into the dark. He couldn't see where the tunnel led, but he knew they needed to get farther back and away from the entrance if they hoped to remain hidden from anyone coming in.

He heard something.

Not from outside—a faint, almost ghostlike rustle floated up from the back of the cave. *What was that?* He imagined ACF scouts that had somehow snuck in before the three of them had entered; he imagined some sort of animal. His body tensed.

"There," he hissed. "Did you hear that?"

"What?" Máire and Aral said in unison.

"Back there. In the cave. Listen."

The three froze, their heads cocked.

"I hear something," Aral said. "It's soft."

"Nothing," Máire said, shaking her head.

"Something's back there," Aral said. "Hang on."

She took a step farther into the cave, hunching over as she walked. She held out her hands to avoid bumping into anything.

"Wait!" Rex snapped. "Don't! It could be ACF or something, don't you think?"

"Impossible," Aral said. "The only thing out here are rodents—that's all I've ever seen. But *that* doesn't sound like a rodent—not like one I've ever heard. It sounds like . . . " her voice trailed off.

"Like what?" Rex asked.

"*Hang on*. Remember: I'm the only one of us who grew up here." Aral's voice had a new emotion in it—one Rex hadn't sensed from her before. She sounded as if she were teasing him. In the gloom, he couldn't make out her facial expressions, but her tone made it sound as if she was even smiling.

Turning away from the two Ætherians, Aral worked her feet over the porous rock underfoot. Even though she was out of sight of the cave's mouth, there was enough light for her to make out the winding tunnel in front of her. Down, down, she went, leaning backward as the slope increased. Every few steps, she paused, listening. The rustle had grown louder, and from outside, still no noise. She was close. With the sound this close, Aral felt her fear evaporate and be replaced by a nervous excitement. The closer she got, the more certain she grew of what she was hearing.

To keep from falling, she soon had to lean back and place her hands on the cave floor, her fingertips gripping into the cavities in the rock. It was rough to the touch. Step, step, step . . . Before advancing each time, she planted a foot squarely on the rock and tested her grip. Only then would she ease her next foot down, down . . .

"Ah!" she cried out as her feet slipped from under her. With a painful thud, her bottom smacked against the rock, and she rolled as she fell, her arms, hands, and legs lacerating as they scraped across the jagged surface. Pain shot through her battered limbs. The thought flashed through her mind that she might plummet to her death here in the dark, and there was nothing anybody could do about it.

As soon as her fall had begun, it was over. With a jolt, her feet splashed down into a frigid liquid, and a cold unlike anything she'd ever felt shot up her legs and through her spine. Her palms and arms may have stung from scrapes and throbbed from being beaten by the rock, but she ignored the pain and leaned forward, plunging her hand into the liquid. Here, a faint sliver of light allowed her to make out the general shape of the cavern she'd fallen into. She couldn't see the liquid, but to the touch it felt pure and clean. Whatever it was, it was flowing through the cavern as an underground stream, rustling and bubbling as it passed through. It seemed deep.

Forming a cup with her hand, Aral scooped up some of the liquid and lifted it to her nose. She smelled. There was no odor.

She took a breath and calmed her trembling hand, which she held to her lips.

She sipped.

She held the liquid in her mouth.

She swallowed.

With a rush of euphoria, she looked back up the slope and began scrambling her way back to the others.

She now understood why she'd seen dried plants, shrubs, and sticks scattered around Cthonia. She understood why she'd heard mosquitoes more than once during her time as a spotter. She'd always assumed that Cthonia's surface was completely barren, dry—an environment hostile to plants and insects. But now she understood.

She'd found water.

EIGHT

THE TEAM OF CTHONIANS EDGED TOWARD the smoldering airship.

Behind them, the injured Ætherians lay on their backs, faces exposed, their eyes staring in wonder at the world around them. The Cthonians, seeing that their enemies' wounds were not fatal, had left them on the sand to pursue the remaining Ætherians, who had taken cover behind the flames.

After the initial terror of having their SCRMs removed, the Ætherians felt the pain of their wounds fade at the euphoria of breathing air denser than anything they'd ever breathed. Even compared to the oxygen in their tanks, the Cthonian air felt purer, more life-giving, more natural. Their injuries prevented them from getting up, but their minds became clearer than they'd ever been. Breathing this air was almost like a drug—it made them feel light, clement, and, surprisingly, no longer hostile to the Cthonians who'd attacked them.

In the moment the Cthonian air brought fresh oxygen to their organs and cells, they also realized they no longer knew what was what. For their entire lives, they'd lived in the stratosphere with the understanding—no, the accepted fact—that Cthonia's air was toxic. They'd always known, as everyone in Ætheria had, that the Cthonians lived down below, but as a primitive race of hermits who survived through respirators. Yet here were the Cthonians in the flesh, and none of them wore masks. And here they were, the Ætherians, breathing the so-called toxic air. The Ætherians were wounded, their bodies were broken, but their minds throbbed with the realization that if the main reason they'd been given for remaining in Ætheria was false, what else was a lie?

———

Leading with his rifle, Tom hesitated before rounding the back of the plane. Because the tail tapered from the machine's belly, a gap remained between it and the ground. Just before he arrived at the space where the Ætherians could see his feet from the other side, he raised his hand for his team to stop. Kneeling, he laid his rifle on the sand and placed his hands on the ground in push-up position. He eased his head forward, his cheek inches above the sand. With heart pounding, he peered under the crack.

At first, all he saw was more of the desert, extending off for miles in the direction of the Cthonian Cave Complex. There was no sign of the Ætherians. If he'd been with them, he wouldn't have waited around either. He would've taken cover in the rocks. Still, he inched forward, and more of the desert revealed itself as the aircraft's tail sloped higher. Beyond, he saw mountains, sand, and, as he eased himself back onto his feet and under the tail, the beginning of the rocky outcropping a mile away.

The Ætherians were gone.

Swearing, he picked up his rifle and motioned for the others to follow. They moved slowly, because now the danger lay not on the other side of the wreck, but in the rocks.

It never occurred to Tom and his soldiers that the Ætherians might slip around the nose of the airship and surprise them from behind.

When the first Stær gun charge hit, it was too late.

Ziiiiiiip!

A crack and an electric buzz jolted the air, popping above the sound of the fire.

In one shot, Tom's two tail soldiers fell, their bodies arching and writhing in agony. The others spun around, their hair bristling from the electricity in the air. Facing the outcropping, they at first saw no one—only the wreckage, the debris, and the bodies from before. Then two bursts of sparks up in the rocks revealed that the Ætherians had not only circled the front of the plane like a squirrel running around a tree from a fox, but they had climbed halfway up the bluff and hidden in the trench the Cthonians had passed when they had fled for cover earlier.

How did they get up so fast? Tom caught himself thinking as the new Stær charges hurtled at them, zipping through the air.

This time, the Ætherians missed. The energy charges thudded into the sand and the side of the airship, just shy of the open fuselage door. Like miniature bolts of lightning, bluish-white arcs buzzed and zapped across the frame as the Stær shot discharged one hundred thousand volts into the metal. Before the Cthonians could react, a third burst of sparks popped from the trench and sent a hissing charge flying at them.

"Ahhh!" Three more Cthonians fell to the

ground, but unlike the others and Rex, they didn't thrash when they were hit. They fell motionless in a heap as the zaps of electricity popped over them.

Seeing his soldiers fall, Tom felt a rush of panic.

"Pull back and fire! Get out of range!" he screamed, lifting his rifle to his shoulder and pulling the trigger. Firing their weapons every few steps, the soldiers formed a line and shuffled backward. They shot in bursts, but they timed their fire so that a nonstop volley of bullets pummeled the rock face. Massive plumes of dust and rock fragments exploded from the bluff, and the *tacktacktacktack* of the gunfire was deafening.

No sooner had the Cthonians opened fire than the Stær gunshots ceased. Between bursts, Tom peered at the trench line over his sights. No movement or human silhouette interrupted the undulating rocks. The Ætherians must've dropped down for cover, just as the Cthonians had earlier. Given the difference in their weapons, Tom had at first thought it had been suicidal for the Ætherians to try and ambush them. He had thought they must've been desperate. Now the Ætherians had already felled five of his soldiers, and all they'd been able to do was add even more pockmarks to the pitted rock face that leered at them.

Tom released his trigger. He raised his hand and waved for the others to cease fire. He scanned the scene: should they take cover behind the airship as the Ætherians had done, or should they just run and get out of range? They were already well over fifty yards away, but he'd seen that the range of the Ætherians' weapons was longer. But how long? He didn't want to lose them from sight, but he also didn't want to risk his soldiers' lives . . . especially if some of the Stær gun charges were strong enough to kill a person. Which is what he feared most.

"Back!" he shouted over the thundering silence. "Behind the airship!"

The Cthonians broke into a sprint toward the wreck. As they ran, more charges flew at them, throwing up the sand around them amid sparks and jolts of electricity. Unharmed, they rounded the back of the plane and hurried to the other side. The burning shell was now between them and the Ætherians.

"Look," one of the soldiers said to Tom, pointing toward the rocks on this side. "The trench!"

Tom cast a fearful glance toward the front of the airship and the bluff. They may have been able to escape the Ætherians' immediate onslaught, he thought, but in seconds it would begin again, for the trench spanned several hundred yards. All the Ætherians would have to do would be to move westward and . . .

"Get behind the airship!" Tom roared. "Behind the tail! Now! We're still open!"

The soldiers slid back, but Tom knew all the Ætherians would have to do was split into two groups on either side of the airship's nose. Then they would have the Cthonians trapped in crossfire. There would be little they could do to mount a real defense.

Just as the beleaguered team reached the tail, a new sound rose over that of the crackling fire and the zips of the Stær projectiles. Someone was shouting—someone over in the rocks. Was it the Ætherians? Hector's team? What were they saying? Tom strained to hear, but could only make out two or three voices that seemed to be barking orders. He could distinguish no words. What were the Ætherians planning?

"Tom, are you there?!" a Cthonian's voice boomed. The sudden shout caused Tom to flinch. His soldiers remained alert. Half kept their rifles pointed down the right side of the plane—the other half, the left side.

"What is it?" he shouted back. "Where *are* you?" Tom's voice quivered as he screamed out his words.

"It's okay!" the voice sounded euphoric. "You can come out! We've got them covered! They've dropped their weapons. Come out!"

Tom nodded to the others to fall out. They filed around the right side of the plane and spread out, sweeping their rifles left and right, ready for a new assault. None came.

Up ahead, Tom saw the thirteen silhouettes of his soldiers standing in a line across the top of the ridge. They held their rifles pointed downward, where more than twenty Ætherian ACF scouts stood with their hands raised and their backs to the rock. They'd been caught from behind, just as Tom and his men had been caught by the Ætherians minutes before. Tom couldn't help but chuckle under his breath at the irony, but seeing the Ætherians now, he remembered Máire's plan. They were still wearing their masks. As Tom and his team approached, he shouted toward the rocks.

"Do you see any Ætherian casualties?" he shouted.

"Six are dead—here in the trench."

From where he stood, Tom could see a few of his soldiers point down. He then glanced around. The wounded Ætherians were still lying in the sand, breathing slowly but deeply. He looked at the fallen Cthonians.

"Quick," he said to the soldiers standing with him. "Let's check our guys and see what's going on."

Tom stepped up to one of the prostrate soldiers and knelt. It was one of the pilots. He was lying on his back, eyes closed. If Tom hadn't seen him get hit by the Stær blast, he would've thought the man was sleeping. The pilot looked peaceful, relaxed. Tom reached forward and placed two fingers on his neck. He felt a pulse. He looked up and saw that two other soldiers were kneeling by the other fallen Cthonians. They gave Tom a thumbs-up. The soldiers were alive. Tom let out a sigh. They'd only been stunned, after all.

"You three," he said, indicating the two kneeling soldiers and a third, "stay with our guys. You two," he pointed to two others, "check the wounded Ætherians and keep guard."

Tom stood and looked eastward, in the direction of the other airship and the impact site. What he saw didn't surprise him, but seeing it stirred him back into feverish action. About a half mile away, a line of hundreds of black human silhouettes were bearing down on them. The Ætherians were coming.

NINE

"ONE BY ONE, ÆTHERIANS, GET DOWN here!" Tom bellowed, his rifle pointed up the slope of the rock face. "Hurry! And don't forget: you're covered on both sides!"

"Go on, move!" one of the soldiers echoed from above. Though the Cthonians were now outnumbered by almost ten, it would've been impossible for the Ætherians to fight back from their position. They were trapped. Twenty armed Cthonians loomed above them, while twenty kept their weapons trained on them from below.

Like crabs scurrying down a hill, the Ætherians

climbed down the rock face. Because the bluff was so steep, they had to shimmy down backward, gripping the surface with both hands and feet. Tom shook his head at how ridiculous they looked. Each was wearing a black, skintight uniform like Rex's, and each wore one of those bulky rubber masks. On their backs, a small oxygen canister was attached. *How could they see through those things? How can they even breathe?* Tom shuddered at the thought of having something like that wrapped around his head and face. He also couldn't fathom how they'd been able to come all the way down from Ætheria wrapped up like that, much less engage in a firefight. He partly felt impressed by the Ætherians' agility with such cumbersome equipment.

"Over there," he said as the Ætherians reached the sand. "Form a line. On your knees and put your hands on your head." He pointed off to his right. Several of his soldiers spread out and pointed to a spot for the first Ætherian to kneel. "And keep your eyes on that wreck!" Tom shouted as their prisoners lined up. He didn't want them to see the other Ætherians that were coming and get inspired to fight back.

With all the Ætherians lined up on their knees, the Cthonians up above followed suit. They scrambled down one at a time so that the others could keep their rifles trained on the Ætherians. As for the prisoners, they didn't speak or make any other noise. Because their faces were covered, it was impossible to see their expressions. Were they afraid? Panicked? Relaxed? Or spiteful?

When all of the Cthonians soldiers had reached the sand, all but three stood behind the Ætherians.

Tom stepped forward and spoke.

"Can you understand me? Nod if you can."

There was a moment of hesitation. The ACF seemed frozen in place. Then, one by one, they exchanged glances through their goggles and nodded.

"Good," Tom continued. "Before he got shot,

did any of you speak to the man whose mask got pulled off? Did he say anything to you?"

No one answered.

"Come on! Speak up! He didn't have a mask on. Did *that* kill him? Did it?! Look at me! Look at all of us!" He pointed to the Cthonian soldiers. "Did you ever wonder why *we* don't have masks on! Look!" He opened his mouth wide and took in several large gulps of air. He exaggerated his shoulder movement. "You've been living up there," he nodded toward the yellowish Welcans cloud above, "and how much air do you have up there to breathe, huh?"

He stepped in closer and pointed back up to the rocky trench.

"If your man hadn't been shot, he'd still be here with you, breathing. Over there." He pointed to where his three soldiers were standing with the wounded Ætherians. "Over there, you've got two of your guys who've been wounded. My men are with them now. And guess what? We took off their masks!" He looked over to one of the guards near the airship.

"Soldier!" he shouted.

"Sir!"

"Is that Ætherian still alive?"

"Yes sir!"

"How's his breathing?"

"Fine! He can speak!"

"Can he? Have him shout something out to his teammates over here."

There was a pause, followed by a high-pitched, shaky voice—one Tom didn't recognize. It was the Ætherian.

"It's Dalar, Tracker ID number 1031! I've been shot in the thigh! But I can breathe! My mask has been off this whole time! I can breathe!" Despite the strain in his voice, it contained a hint of exhilaration.

Hearing their comrade speak had a visible effect on the Ætherians. Their bodies wavered as they glanced back and forth at each other. No one person seemed to be the focus of their attention. Tom assumed this was because their leader Roman had been killed in the firefight. The faceless Ætherians seemed confused, stunned, and unsure of what to do.

"Take off your masks," Tom said, stepping back so that he could scan the entire row of prisoners.

The Ætherians froze, their goggles all pointed at Tom.

"I'll say it again. My soldiers are all standing behind you. Their rifles are aimed at your backs. You saw up there what those weapons can do. Now, take off your masks. Do it, or I will give them the order to fire."

The Ætherians didn't move.

"Alright, so be it. Everyone, clear out." The Cthonians in front of the Ætherians walked to the side of the column to get out of the way of the bullets that would come from their own soldiers.

Schloop.

With the sound of a rubber suction cup being

removed from a smooth surface, an Ætherian near the middle of the line yanked her own mask off and let it dangle beside her.

"Wait!" she shouted, her eyes wide with terror. Tom paused. The unmasked Ætherian took her first gulps of Cthonian air and, as with the others, her face gained color and her eyes burned with a new energy. The former terror of battle and death was replaced by ecstasy and bliss.

"Oh, my God," she muttered in between breaths. "I can breathe. It's true." She took in several more breaths, trying to extend her lungs all the way down to her navel. She breathed in so deeply, she felt she would burst. With each breath, oxygen saturated every cell of her body.

One by one, the others pulled off their masks, revealing sweaty, pale, yet vivified and euphoric faces. After a few breaths, they began talking to each other at once. Their entire demeanor had changed. Before, they'd been nimble and pugnacious soldiers in what they thought was a hostile environment.

Now, they babbled like children about to receive a new toy.

"Ætherians, stop!" Tom shouted over the din. The ACF fell silent, but their eyes continued to sparkle. "Can you understand now why Rex tried to pull off your man's mask? Do you understand?"

Some of the Ætherians' mouths moved as if they wanted to say something, but no words came out. Spiraling thoughts and conflicting truths overwhelmed their oxygen-saturated minds. Some even seemed to be suppressing giggles. As Tom spoke, they recalled the scene from less than thirty minutes ago.

"*You* shot him!" Tom continued. "We were watching! Do you understand now that we were defending him? We did *not* want to fight you! And we do *not* want to fight you!"

The Ætherians gaped at him. Tom turned to one of the soldiers.

"Hector, go get the others. In the cave. I think

now it would be a better idea for them to see who we've got hidden up there."

Hector hesitated before moving, perplexed. Had Tom changed his plan? Hector had thought that Máire, Aral, and Rex were supposed to stay out of sight because they were the only ones unarmed. Then he realized why: Máire and Rex were Ætherians.

"Yes sir!" he snapped, running off toward the rocky incline. Like a rapt audience, the Ætherians kept their eyes on Hector as he ran up and disappeared into the second cave mouth. Some voices and scuffling emerged from within. It sounded as if Hector was having to convince the three fugitives to come out into the open. He must've been persuasive, because a few seconds later, he reemerged, followed by Aral, Máire, and Rex.

The Ætherians let out an audible gasp when they saw Rex. He was the reason they'd been sent down in the first place—that, and to search for food and water. Here he was: Ætheria's number one fugitive, walking toward them as if nothing were wrong. As if he hadn't committed a felony by helping the Cthonian prisoner escape. As if he hadn't just assaulted Roman, their Point, by yanking off his mask. As if he weren't suspected by the Head Ductor himself of somehow being connected to the original attack on the Proboscis.

The moments these thoughts struck, they were overpowered by the one unavoidable truth: the main story the Head Ductor had told them about their entire existence in Ætheria—that only in Ætheria could they breathe—had been a lie. If that had been a lie, what else was a lie? They had been *told* that Rex was an escaped fugitive . . . but was that true? They had been *told* that Aral was identified as an enemy of the state . . . but was that true? They had been *told* that the Cthonian attack on the Proboscis had been an unprovoked assault on the Ætherian civilization.

But was that true?

As the Ætherians wrestled with their thoughts,

their sparkling eyes shifted from Rex to the other Ætherian walking in front of him. Who was she? What was she doing here? Why was she with Rex? Could she have helped him escape? What if he hadn't escaped, after all?

The three followed Hector down the slope and across the sand. Rex, Máire, and Aral never took their eyes off of the Ætherians. Rex scanned each of their faces to see if he recognized anyone, but he didn't. Aral also looked into their features for anyone she may have seen during her interrogation and forced Sanatorium stay. Despite the presence of the armed Cthonians, the three couldn't shake their nervous dread. They, too, knew the ACF swarms were minutes away.

"Can you talk to them?" Tom asked Máire. "Tell them your story. That might help."

Without hesitating, Máire nodded and stepped up to the center of the Ætherians and planted her feet in the sand. With intense features, she glared at them—not in a menacing way, but rather in a commanding way.

"You may not know who I am," she began, "but I'll tell you. And you may not believe me, but so be it. In the end, you'll have to choose who you'll believe. And you'll have to do so fast."

Over the next few minutes, Máire told her story, from beginning to end. Knowing that the other Ætherians were not far off, she spoke quickly but confidently, ending by revealing the name of her husband: Stan Leif.

As she finished, the Ætherians remained silent.

"Oh, you don't know that name? Who would? Everyone else calls him the Head Ductor!"

Gasps.

"What?"

"How?"

"You can't . . . "

"Prove it!"

"And this," Máire pointed to Rex, "is *his* son Rex—the very baby I had to leave behind. Maybe you've heard of Rex's foster father: Franklin Strapp? He was killed in the attack on the Proboscis!"

"I knew him," one of the Ætherians at the end of the line said. "I was assigned as part-time Protector in Tátea. He and I spoke just a few times, but . . ."

"Yes?"

"I remember him mentioning a son, but no one ever saw him."

"So here's another thing," Máire continued. "Have you ever noticed that *only* members of the Ætherian High Command wear oxygen canisters on their backs? Have you?"

Nods.

"Any ideas why?" She didn't let them answer. "I'll tell you why! You saw how strong you felt when you breathed the air down here? That should be a lesson as to how weak and oxygen-deprived you were up there! Of course you never realized it because you had nothing to compare it to. But now . . . if you knew that the oxygen the Council members wear all the time was just as pure as the air down here, now you know that they have been keeping you weak while they stay strong." She jabbed her hand skyward. "For years, Stan—the HD—had actually been pulling fresh oxygen up through the Proboscis and hoarding it. Not only is there enough up there for everyone, there's *no need* to stay up there! You're putting your lives at risk for what? So that one man can control you? He's a monster!"

The Ætherians erupted into a confused, rattled chatter. They'd never heard anyone speak like this about the Head Ductor, who was always referred to in hushed tones and with language of respect and deference. Aside from the truth that they could now breathe the Cthonian air, there was something reassuring in Máire's confidence. Their world was being turned upside down, and they felt paralyzed.

"And now," Máire continued. "Now the Proboscis is cut and the Ætherians have no natural gas, no fresh air, and no water. How much longer until you all die up there?!"

"But *we* do," Aral spoke up from Máire's left.

"Yes, listen to her—to what she has just found!" Máire said, holding her hand out to motion to Aral.

"Back there," Aral began, "in that cave, while we were hiding . . . I found an underground river of fresh water. I don't know how deep it is. But there's a lot of it flowing through there. Back where we're from," she pointed west, "we had an aquifer. Just like this one—like the one you've been drawing from. But ours dried up. We had come to you looking for water. Only one man—one of our generals—who thought his son had been murdered by Ætherians . . . he was blinded by a personal vendetta against you—*he's* the one who cut your pipe. *Not* the Cthonians. Even our command sent orders for him *not* to attack—I saw them. You have to understand: it was *one* man—not all of us! The Cthonians have *never* wanted to harm the Ætherians!"

Tom reacted visibly to Aral's revelation. When he'd spoken with her before taking off in the airship earlier, she'd told him how the general had ordered the severing of the tube and how he'd miscalculated the charges, igniting a cthoneum gas pocket and destroying his entire Command Post and Ætheria's Power Works at the same time. But she'd never openly denounced the entire operation as *his* decision. As for the command's orders not to attack, he hadn't seen those either. All he knew was that his orders had been to fly out to the site with his soldiers and Máire and try to recover what they could.

"There's another thing you should know," Rex spoke up, facing the Ætherians. "When I came down before with Unit Alif, we saw the Cthonian plane, and my Stær gun malfunctioned. It misfired and *they*—the Cthonians—thought we'd shot at them. But it's not true! It was an accident! You *have* to believe us!"

Tom gave another start at Rex's confession, his eyes wide and his mouth open.

"So now *you* have to decide," Máire continued. "Your reinforcements are almost here. And ours are on the way. But neither side *really* wants war.

Everyone's overreacting because of wrong conclusions. So what are you going to do? Let the ACF incapacitate us all? Take us prisoner? Then what? Go back up to Ætheria, now that you know the truth? What will you do up there, next time you see a Council member with their bottled oxygen? Will *you* say nothing? Will *you* do nothing? Now that you've tasted the air down here, how can you even *think* about returning back to a willful state of hypoxia—forever oxygen-deprived and sluggish, just because your leadership wants it that way.

"So decide!"

TEN

"**M**AY WE STAND UP?" ONE OF THE Ætherians asked. Calm filled her voice, but she was still trying to contain the ebullience of such pure oxygen for the first time in her life. She spoke with a voice of honesty—a voice that had been given new life by new air.

Tom shot a glance at his soldiers. They looked at him for direction.

"Go ahead," he said. "Remember, we're watching you. What do you want to do?"

"Let us talk to them," the Ætherian said, standing up. "When Roman had his mask pulled off, I thought he'd be dead. That happened, just not the way we thought." The others joined her, shaking the pins and needles from their legs as she and Tom spoke. A winsome giddiness infected them all. Their new demeanor was not one of soldiers who'd just survived a deadly battle. It was one of exhilaration and joy. It was the demeanor of people who'd just learned that their reasons for fighting were all wrong.

"What's your name?"

"Pace."

"Okay, Pace," Tom said. "How?"

Pace turned to the other Ætherians and spoke to no one in particular. Tom had the impression she was thinking aloud—forming her plan as she spoke—but that she was making a point to speak so that both the Cthonians and the Ætherians could hear.

"When they get here, let us go to them. They'll see us first. They'll see we aren't wearing masks. If we can get them to take their masks off, we . . . " her voice trailed off.

"What?" Tom asked.

"We might start a revolution if two hundred ACF realize the truth about Ætheria. All we'd have to do is get back up top and tell everyone else. If they believe us, the game is up."

Tom thought. He glanced back toward the rocks. Should he believe the Ætherians? Could they just be setting him up for a trap? Should he try to make it up into the rocks and take cover, as he'd originally planned? He looked eastward. The Ætherians were just under a hundred yards away—they were now so close he could make out the circular glint in their mask goggles. They all had their Stær guns drawn. Torn, he looked back at the rocks. There was no way his team would be able to get up there and out of sight before the Ætherians would be on top of them. Even if they could get hidden, he wasn't sure the Cthonians had enough ammunition to maintain a firefight long enough for their reinforcements to arrive the following day. With that many approaching Ætherians, they were outgunned five to one.

"Okay, Pace, listen," he said. "Let's do it. But we're not letting go of our weapons, do you understand? We'll stand back twenty yards. If a fight breaks out again, we may all die, but know that you'll die with us—and first of all."

"Agreed," Pace said. She turned to the other thirty-odd Ætherians and nodded. The Ætherians stood together while the Cthonians, Máire, and Rex lined up behind them.

From his vantage point, Rex could peer past the individual, unmasked Ætherians and see their comrades were now less than fifty yards away. His heartbeat quickened as they approached. There was something about their skintight AG suits and their masks that gave them an alien, almost monstrous quality. This was made even more sinister by their Stær guns, which were drawn and aimed in Rex's and the others' direction. Like robots, the ACF looked identical in their uniforms. It was impossible to recognize anyone.

The new Ætherians slowed as they approached. They stopped. Puzzled, they rotated their heads erratically at the exposed Ætherian faces looking at them.

If Pace and the others had originally planned to parley between two warring factions, any hope of a calm discussion vanished the moment they turned away from the Cthonians and toward the approaching Ætherians.

As if on cue, the unmasked Ætherians rushed their masked counterparts, shouting and tittering with delight. The sudden movement startled the Cthonians, who raised their weapons in alarm. No sooner had they prepared to fire in self-defense than they realized they had not been betrayed. Each of the unmasked Ætherians darted among the troops, each trying to be the first to reveal the news to their comrades. From among the chatter, volleys of "You won't believe it," "It's true, it's true," "Just try," "We thought so, too," and "Look at us!" filled the air. The Cthonians relaxed their grips on their weapons, but remained alert.

As the unmasked Ætherians hurriedly repeated what Tom, Máire, Aral, and Rex had revealed to them, the masked Ætherians' Stær guns began to lower. Goggled masks shifted from looking at Pace and the others to the Cthonians, who shifted in place nervously.

Then, one by one, the Stær guns found their way back into their holsters and, one by one, the army of Ætherians removed their SCRMs and dropped them to their sides.

One by one, they filled their lungs with their first taste of oxygen. In their euphoria, they rushed the Cthonians—not in attack, but in the desire to thank them for revealing this new truth to them. In their minds, the Ætherians already felt liberated, free. They felt free from the oppressive state of permanent hypoxia that kept their energy sluggish and brutish. They felt free from worry about being constantly monitored through their Trackers. They felt free from the claustrophobic life on their limited islands above the clouds, where the slightest misstep could get you Tossed.

"ACF!" one Protector finally shouted above the din, silencing the scouts. Still giddy on the life-giving rush of oxygen, they struggled to contain their smiles as they turned to listen to their Point. "We have air here! Air!"

The Ætherians shouted in elation. Some clapped. Some catcalled. But the Point's countenance quickly fell as her mind flew through what she really knew, and what she now needed to reveal.

"There's something else you all should know!" she continued. "Ætheria's running out of water stores. Our generators don't have much life left. When they die, all of the heating in the community centers will go. After that, it's just three or four days before the inside temperatures match the outside. That's sixty below."

"But I thought we had enough to last for two weeks?" Rex said.

"That's what you were *told*," she responded dryly.

"How do *you* know that?" Máire asked.

"My name is Ama. I was in a meeting with the Head Ductor and the rest of the Ætherian High Command." She paused and looked around. "No one's supposed to know. I was sworn to secrecy. Why do you think so many of us were sent down? And why do you think our mission was not just to secure the site and find Rex, but to *look for signs of life*? To look for water and food? Didn't that seem strange to any of you?" She paused, shaking her head. "As it is, I'd be surprised if at least some people back home didn't suspect what was going on, even if they didn't want to admit it to themselves."

Ama's words had an immediate effect on the other Ætherians. Now that they knew the truth about Cthonia, and with the ever-looming threat of their water stores and electricity generators ceasing to keep them alive, they realized that they had to act. Most of them had families and friends scattered throughout the archipelago—family and friends who would surely die if a solution to Ætheria's crisis was not found soon. Their earlier elation gave way to angry but frightened grumbling. A few voices shouted over the others.

Expressions of joy gave way to expressions of concern and then panic.

"My mom . . . "

"My sons . . . "

"I have to get back . . . "

"Get them out . . . "

"We need to do something—get them down here. We need to hurry!"

"What are you going to do?" Tom asked the Ætherians, sensing their growing worry.

"We have to tell them up top, Ama," Pace said, looking at one of the freshly unmasked ACF. Rex noticed from the scout's chest patch that she was a Point, like Yoné.

Ama nodded, looking the Cthonians over. Her face was still a blend of shock and wonder. "Yes. But . . . " She turned around and looked in the direction of their Power Works's ruins. "If we winch back up in the harnesses and use the descent pods, it will take a full day. Maybe more. We're not scheduled to be back for another three days. They'll suspect something's wrong. What we need to do is find a way to get the word out to as many people in Ætheria at once. Show them. Tell them. And we can't risk the remaining ACF up top suspecting something and stopping us as we trickle up. I don't like it."

"Even if you could get up and talk to people, why would they believe you?" Rex asked. "You and I know because we've been here. Mom knows because she's been here . . . she's *lived* here. We've all breathed the air. We've *felt* it. So have the Cthonians. But back home? If you had told me before I ever came down that I could pull off my mask and not die, I would've thought you were crazy."

"You're right," Ama said. "We would need to get a message to them at once—all of us. Not bit by bit. And to everyone."

"Why don't you radio up?" Tom asked. "Our radios are fried, so I can't contact the CCC for any help." He lifted his receiver from his belt as to prove that he wasn't lying.

Ama shook her head. "Won't work. We've never been able to get any kind of signals through *that*." Ama jabbed her thumb upward in the direction of the Welcans cloud. "That cloud is made of fermionic lithium. That means *nothing* gets through it—no radio, no radar, no infrared, nothing. The only way to get any kind of message is in person. Once we are above the cloud, we could speak into these." She held up her wrist to show her Tracker. "They're monitored. All the time. But still, only a small group of people are listening in at any one time."

Ama paused and looked around, frowning. Her eyes scanned the dry Cthonian landscape for clues— for an idea that would save them.

"No," she continued. "The only way I can think of is to show up in such a dramatic way that it would force the Ætherians to listen. If we could really give them a taste of what's down here, and get to them quickly, maybe then we could convince them. And if we can convince them, maybe then an uprising would . . . "

"Look!" Aral screamed, her voice splitting from the effort. The Cthonians and Ætherians jumped in alarm, lifting their weapons as a group and whipping around left and right, searching. But they saw nothing—no enemy, no threats, no difference.

"What is it?!" Tom howled, anger in his voice.

"There! There!" Aral lifted her arm and pointed skyward.

Rex and the others looked up, as did the Ætherians. At first all he saw was the same roiling mass of the yellowish Welcans cloud—the same he'd seen from above all his life.

"Oh, my God," one of the Cthonians muttered.

"Do you see it?"

"No . . . "

"Is that really there?"

"How could it be?"

"Is it true?"

The Cthonians stood dumbstruck, their eyes glued on one spot in the Welcans cloud. There, the churning, billowing fermionic lithium had broken open, revealing a glimpse of blue sky beyond. As the gap opened up, a hundred-yard-wide ray of sunlight burst through, casting a massive blotch of pure light upon the Cthonian sand a mile away. Like a spotlight, the sunbeam swept across the landscape before disappearing just as quickly behind the clouds.

"No!" Tom shouted, scanning the rest of the sky frantically. Seeing the sunlight—something none of the Cthonians had ever seen before—both stunned and frightened them. Even Aral was amazed. As a prisoner in Ætheria, she'd only ever been outside at night, and during the day she'd been kept in windowless rooms.

In their shock, the Cthonians dropped their rifles and began scouring the sky, looking for other sunbreaks. Even the Ætherians seemed amazed. Though they had spent their entire lives in sunlight so intense it would burn the skin of a Cthonian within minutes, they too had only ever known the Welcans cloud to be a solid, impenetrable mass of toxic lithium.

"My dream . . . " Rex muttered, his eyes glued on the fleeting splotch of blue between the clouds.

"What?" Aral said, facing him.

"Right before I hurt my shoulder. Back in the dormitory. I had a dream. I was walking across Cthonia and I saw this on the ground." Rex spread his arms to create space among the ACF scouts and the Cthonian spotters. As they stepped back and formed a round clearing ten feet across, Rex traced a pattern in the sand with his heel:

"I know that," Aral said, pointing to the triangle. "But that one's upside-down. See?" She lifted her right sleeve to reveal a muscular deltoid muscle. A large tattoo snaked its way across her pale flesh in dark blue ink:

"We all have these," she said. "Everyone in Cthonia gets one when they turn sixteen. It's an ancient symbol for the cthonean element—the ground that provides us with everything. Or at least that used to provide us . . . "

"Yeah, I saw them on the others. The bodies up there. In the morgue. And on your eqūs animals. I just assumed the symbol meant 'Cthonian' or something like that. And when I saw this in my dream, I had no idea what was going on. But now I get it. The circles are the sun. They have to be, can't you see? The Cthonian order is turned upside-down as the sun comes out from behind the cloud. It has to be!"

"Wait a second," one of the airship pilots interrupted. "If that's a break in the cloud . . . then that means no bad weather up there—at least right there in the spot. No turbulence . . . " he squinted and shielded his eyes from the glaring light that was pushing through the cloud break. "From here it looks at least one or two hundred yards wide, but is it closing?" He let his hand drop. "That could mean . . . if it's closing, we'd have to hurry, or else . . . "

His voice trailed off. And with a new glint in his eye, he turned to face the slumbering airship where Aral and Rex had hidden the night before.

ELEVEN

BACK IN ÆTHERIA, WORK ON THE PROBOSCIS was advancing, but not fast enough for the Head Ductor and the rest of the archipelago's population.

Their time was running out.

Soon after the Cthonians' unprovoked attack it was decided the new Power Works would be constructed on Tátea, near where the previous one had been. By now the remaining rubble had been cleared away, leaving a charred, flat expanse fifty yards wide.

But the new Power Works would not be on the

exact same site. The southeastern tip of Tátea had been blown off in the explosion, leaving a massive crater. Viewed from above or below, Tátea looked like an enormous cookie out of which a giant had taken a greedy bite. Ætherian engineers were now too unsure about the structural integrity of that part of the island to risk placing another construction there—especially one so vital to Ætherians' survival. So they chose the western side, midway up.

On the day the unmasked ACF and the Cthonian forces united below the Welcans cloud, fifty Ætherian workers teemed over the construction site on Tátea. The foundation for the new Power Works had already been laid, and the structure's teardrop-shaped skeleton had taken shape. As for the new Proboscis, it extended a mile downward, stopping just above the Welcans cloud like the stinger on a giant wasp. Inside the tube, dozens of workers—some volunteers, some engineers, some construction workers—welded and bolted together the pieces of Ætheria's lifeline. Each person was strapped in by a tecton harness affixed either to the Proboscis itself or the underside of Tátea.

That day, work had been proceeding steadily. Though the workers were behind the schedule set by the Head Ductor, there had been no wind since sunrise. This allowed them to make twice the progress they'd make on a windy day, which was always more dangerous as the gale threatened to dash the harnessed workers into the Proboscis.

At this height, the workers—and all Ætherians—were used to the sounds of the stratosphere: howling airstreams, thunder from below, or the muffled *swoosh* of far-off winds on a calm day.

But today, just an hour before sunset, the workers at the bottom mouth of the Proboscis paused in their welding. Somewhere below the Welcans cloud, something was happening. A new sound floated up to them through the fermionic lithium. The first workers to hear it shook their heads and kept working, assuming their ears had deceived them. When the sound reappeared and became more constant, droning, and high-pitched over the far-off breezes and their own breathing, the workers turned off their acetylene torches and held their breath, listening.

Something down below was whining. The whine didn't fluctuate, but soon a low-pitched grumble appeared underneath the sustained high note. In sonority, it reminded the workers of thunder, but unlike thunder that burst and faded, this growl rumbled and shook with a growing intensity. The growl became a snarl, and then the snarl, a roar.

The noise was directly under them, and it was coming closer.

Because all of the workers' eyes were now glued on the roiling Welcans cloud below, they all saw what happened next.

Like a whale or a shark erupting from a turbulent ocean, a titanic machine exploded through the fermionic lithium, parting the yellowish cloud and sending swirling wisps of the toxic gas spurting upward. The machine was silver and round, but on either side, two screaming turbines clutched onto flattened wings. The turbines were round and black in the middle. Their deafening howling made the Ætherian workers snatch their hands to their ears as their heartbeats quickened in panic. At the back of the machine, two smaller wings formed an upside-down T with what looked like a fin sticking straight up.

The machine rose. The Ætherians, feeling exposed at the end of their ropes like fish bait on hooks, kicked and flailed about, trying to climb back up and away from the approaching monstrosity.

The fully-loaded Cthonian airship had come to Ætheria.

With a mixture of terror and wonder, the Ætherian workers gawked at the rising aircraft. Until that moment, the largest apparatus any of them had ever seen had been the machinery inside the destroyed Power Works. Even that had not made a noise anywhere near the screaming that now rattled their skulls. What was it? Where had it come from? Where was it going? Who—or what—was in it? Only a few of the workers realized it must've been a Cthonian transport, though none of them could've guessed that the only Cthonians on board were the pilots. Everyone else was Ætherian.

After bursting through the Welcans cloud, the airship rose until it cleared Tátea's surface. There, it hovered and rotated. Like a huge cyclop's eye, the glassy cockpit windshield seemed to be ogling the burned site where the Power Works had once stood. With a scream of its engines, the airship rose another fifty feet and eased forward until it disappeared from the workers' view from below. As it advanced over Tátea, the formidable engine wash whipped dust, ash, and shreds of artificial turf around into miniature yet powerful cyclones.

Once the airship was over the charred, flat expanse, it hovered once more, rotated in place, and eased itself to the island's surface. The suspension in the landing gear contracted to support the craft's weight. As soon as all of the plane's lift had been shifted from the wings to the wheels, the engines' roaring died down, as did the high-pitched whine of the rotating turbine blades.

Before the airship had even touched down on Tátea, what workers who had been milling about had run, harnessing themselves in as fast as they could to the Zipp lines extending from the island's northern and western sides. One by one they zipped away, fleeing to Bernuac HQ, where—through their panicked reports via their wrist Trackers—the Ætherian Council and the Head Ductor had already been informed of the airship's arrival.

As the engines wound down and became silent, the rear loading ramp opened. It was still moving when the entire ACF force swarmed out. They hesitated behind the plane, their eyes turned to Ama. She lifted her wrist to her mouth and spoke into her Tracker. They were above the Welcans cloud; this meant she could transmit.

"Bernuac HQ this is Ama Dukūr, Point ID

number 6876. *We* are in the airship that just landed on Tátea. It was the Cthonians who brought us up—all ACF except for three wounded and eleven dead. The Cthonians are friendly. I repeat: *they are friendly.*"

She took a deep breath and continued. "But right now we have an emergency: please assemble all Ætherians in the community center halls. We have come back with news they must hear. It's for their own survival—for everyone's survival."

She kept her wrist raised as she waited for a reply. A minute passed before her Tracker crackled and a tinny voice sputtered through.

"I'm afraid we can't agree to that, Point 6876. All ACF are to report to Bernuac HQ for immediate debrief with Deputy Head Schlott. She has been informed of your arrival and is en route now. There is no discussion. That is an order."

Ama muttered something inaudible and looked at the others. Rex and Máire stood at her side. As Ama radioed in, Máire couldn't help but allow her eyes to scan the place she'd left sixteen years before. She recognized Tátea, though when she'd seen it last the bulbous Power Works and Proboscis had been clinging over the side that was now shattered away. She had grown up farther north, on Island Eighteen, but when she'd married the Head Ductor, she'd moved in with him in his quarters at the heart of the Ætherian Council Complex. She squinted her eyes and tried to peer north. Even if there were no buildings in between, both the ACC and her home island were too far away to see. She looked back to Ama, whose face was tense with thought.

The ACF Point covered her Tracker with her other hand and shouted above the wind, which was exceptionally light for this altitude.

"ACF, listen up! We will split into six groups! Five will go to the community centers. There you *must* inform every Ætherian you see of the truth. You must also tell them about our own water shortage. They need to know the danger so that they can escape. The other group will go with me to find the Head Ductor.

"Right now, there are a few dozen ACF still in Ætheria. They will try to stop you, since we've been ordered to Bernuac HQ, and they know. But if they do, you are to fire on them at once. They will be armed, but there are twice as many of us. Check your Stær guns now and make sure they are ready."

Ama counted out the six groups. The Ætherians divided themselves up, each person reaching down and turning on their Stær guns as they moved. Some pulled their weapons out of their holsters and inspected the devices more closely. Seeing this reminded Rex of his own failed attempt at firing his Stær gun after it had fallen in the mud of Cthonia.

Rex turned to Ama.

"Ama?" he said.

"Yes?"

"Can we . . . can I join you in your group?"

Ama nodded. She knew why he had asked to come back when they'd loaded the airship down below. She knew what was at stake. She knew he had a need that, for him, was far more important than saving the Ætherians and starting a new civilization. She knew . . .

Rex then turned to Máire. Before he spoke, she too knew what her son was going to say. When he'd told her down below, she knew she couldn't let him do this on his own. She, too, had things she needed to say. She came up for with the same goal as Rex. But she had her own agenda.

"I wanna see . . . I wanna see *him*," he said, his voice wavering.

"I understand, but . . . don't you think we should, I mean, the others?" Máire muttered unconvincingly. "We've got to tell the others. *You've* got to tell them. You are the only one left of the first team that went down."

"I know, but . . . he's . . . never talked to me. I've

never even *seen* him. This might be my only chance. I found you. I at least want to *see* him once."

Máire hesitated, her eyes glimmering with indecision. Part of her knew she also had things she wanted to say to the Head Ductor. But what was the point? To make herself feel better? To show him all the pain he'd caused? To gloat as all of Ætheria learned the truth about Cthonia . . . and about their fictional vertical world? About *him*? Part of her also understood that, no matter what had happened between the HD and her so many years ago, he was still Rex's father. Didn't Rex have a right to see him?

Yet the risks . . .

"I bet we can get you in," Ama said, interrupting Máire's thoughts. Rex noticed that she was still covering her wrist as she spoke.

"What?"

"I'm in the High Command of the ACF and the Ætherian Council. Right now Rex is the most wanted person in Ætheria. All I have to do is report that we've captured him, and I'm sure the HD will call us in right away."

She hesitated, her eyes on Rex. "After all, he thinks you're a criminal. So that means a Tossing, for sure. And the HD always oversees those. Besides, you are his . . . I mean . . . "

Rex looked at Máire and then back to Ama.

"Okay, let's do it," he said.

Ama glanced at Máire, who nodded. Ama uncovered her wrist and spoke into her Tracker. "Bernuac HQ, Ama 6876 again. We have two . . . prisoners with us. Rex and Máire Himmel, fugitives of the ACF. Request permission to bring them to the ACC for immediate surrender to the Head Ductor."

There was another pause, at least three times longer than the first.

"We hear you. The HD has been notified and will receive you in the meeting hall of the ACC. You and your security detail should report immediately."

"I hear you. We are on our way."

Ama covered her wrist and turned to the five

other groups, who were waiting for her to dismiss them. "ACF, listen up! You each need to get to the community centers as instructed. But we first need time to get to the ACC. So give us five minutes before leaving Tátea. And head north and straight toward Bernuac HQ, splitting off *only* after you reach Island Six. Because if you split up now, they'll know right away from your Trackers that you are not following orders. They might get suspicious, and then the HD could lock himself in his quarters. So let's get our timing right!"

She turned to Rex, Máire, and the ten other members of her group.

"When we get there, you two will need to stand in the middle of us. We'll have our Stær guns out. Otherwise they won't believe that you're prisoners."

Rex hesitated. For a brief instant, his previous worries that this could be a trap flared. He let these go. If he and his mother were in a trap, it was too late. They were already in Ætheria and surrounded by armed ACF. Escape this time would be impossible.

"Okay," Rex said. "We're ready. Mom?"

"I'm ready," Máire said.

"Alright," Ama shouted to the team. "Let's go!"

TWELVE

WHEN AMA'S TEAM ARRIVED AT THE Ætherian Council Complex, they were greeted by five ACF who stared with wide eyes at Rex and Máire. Too much was happening too quickly for them to grasp: first the arrival of the Cthonian airship; then the ACF team that had come back two days early; and finally there, walking through the halls they were stationed to guard was the only fugitive the HD had ever demanded personally. All they had been told was that, "The outlaws are coming under ACF cover. The Head Ductor wants them brought to him without delay."

They were given no details. They were given no answers.

Seeing Rex here, now, they wondered if the Tossing would be today or later.

Ama gave them her Nanokepp Card. One of the guards scanned it to check her clearance as High Command, ACF, and Ætherian Council. They then scanned the other Ætherians' cards one by one. Once they had been cleared, one of the five ACC guards, a tall, lanky man, accompanied the group in.

Walking down the ACC main hall as a feigned prisoner, Rex thought back to when he'd been arrested on Tátea. Then, his head had been covered, and he'd been an actual prisoner. Then, he'd been subjected to sonic torture with the nerve-shattering Pulse. Then, he'd met Protector Challies, who turned out to be his savior. Then, he'd thought his mom was gone forever. Then, he hadn't known that his biological father was the most powerful man in Ætheria.

"The Head Ductor is inside," the lanky ACF

guard said when they reached an imposing set of double stratoneum doors at the end of the hall. "You may go in." He pressed a button on the left-hand side of the doors. With a double beep, the doors swung open.

Ama turned to Rex. She hesitated for a millisecond before speaking.

"Okay, Rex. It's time."

Since Máire had told him that his father was still alive, Rex had imagined what this moment would be like. While the airship was bouncing and jostling upward through the Welcans cloud, Rex had closed his eyes and pictured his father: what he would be like, what he would say when he saw Rex, what Rex would say to him . . . Before, he'd imagined his mother's face to help him get down in the descent pod. Now that he'd found her, his father's unknown face had taken her place and helped him manage the terror of the airship being torn apart by the turbulence of the Welcans cloud. In his daydreams, he had worried that he would be too afraid to confront his father, the Head Ductor of Ætheria.

Now, as Ama beckoned him into the ACC's council room, he was surprised to feel an overwhelming calm and sense of relaxation—feelings he hadn't expected. All fear evaporated. It was as if he'd just taken a drug that caused every nerve and muscle in his body to release. Or maybe, given everything he'd been through, he just didn't care.

Rex and Máire stepped through the doors, followed by Ama's team of ACF. The guard closed the doors behind them and stayed outside. As they walked into the room, Ama nodded at two of her scouts. They returned the nod and positioned themselves like two sentries in front of the double doors. Were they planning on keeping people out or in? Rex's eyes lingered on them as his previous fear of walking into a trap flashed through his mind. He let it go and shifted his attention to his new surroundings.

The room was fifteen yards across and circular

with what looked like smooth, concave cabinet doors lining the walls. In the middle sat a large, highly polished, donut-shaped table. Thirty evenly spaced, cushioned chairs sat pushed up against the table. The one opposite the double doors was the largest, its burgundy leather cushion bulging up to the height of a full-grown Ætherian.

Before he could register what was happening, a hissing noise off to the right caught Rex's attention. He turned and saw a short, beady man with greased-back hair. The man's back was turned to the door, and he was standing at one of the wall cabinets, which was open. Hearing the group come in, the man twisted something inside the cabinet, spun around, and slammed the cabinet shut, but not before Rex could see what was inside: stacks and stacks of oxygen canisters like the ones worn by the members of the Ætherian High Command. Their nozzles faced outward. When the man twisted his hand, the hissing stopped. Rex's first thought was that he had been huffing some oxygen from one of the canisters, because he wasn't wearing one himself. He looked at the group, red-faced like a child who'd been caught with his hand in the cookie jar.

"Stan," Máire said in a soft tone, stepping to the front of the group.

The Head Ductor froze, his eyes bulging behind thick glasses.

"Máire?" His voice sounded pinched. "You . . . you're alive? They didn't tell me *you* were coming."

"Meet your son." She ignored his question, gesturing toward Rex, whose eyes had never left Stan Leif's since the Head Ductor had turned around. "The last time you saw him, he was two weeks old."

Stan glanced at Rex and looked back at Máire. His face soured. "I know who he is. I've always known. Who do you think I am?" Stan spoke without looking at Rex. Seeing his biological father, Rex felt no emotion. He felt empty, like an automaton. Even though his foster dad had always been distant, Rex realized now he had felt much more for Franklin Strapp—a man who wasn't even related to him—than this frog of a man standing in front of him now. If anything, all Rex felt was the overwhelming urge to leave . . . to go back down to Cthonia with his mom and form the new family he'd been dreaming of.

Stan looked at Ama. "Good work," he said. "You may leave him and four guards with me. But take *her* into custody. We'll deal with her later."

The other ACF scouts wavered, their Stær guns drawn but pointed downward. They glanced at Ama. Ama stepped forward. A surge of fear coursed through Rex.

"No," Máire said. "Do you know what's happening? *They* know the truth about Cthonia. They know about the air down there. They breathed it, so did he." She pointed to Rex. "*I* have breathed it for sixteen years." She paused, a scowl crossing her face. "But *you* know that."

"What she's trying to say," Ama interrupted, raising her wrist to her mouth so that her Tracker transponder would pick up every word. She knew that no fewer than twenty ACF monitors would hear what she said. "Right now, every ACF scout that went down with us is spreading out to tell all of Ætheria in the community centers that the air on Cthonia is not only breathable, but it is much more dense than the air up here. More than that, they're being told that we're almost out of water and fuel for the generators. That we're going to die if we stay here!"

"And," Máire said, raising her voice so the others' Trackers would hear, "I have told them about you. About how your entire time as Head Ductor has been about hoarding oxygen—about keeping it from Ætherians. You let the Ætherian Council and High Command have oxygen, and why? Because *you* know it gives them life and energy—it lets them think. But that without oxygen, the best all the others can ever hope to be is fifty percent of what they *could* be. But they don't know, so they don't do anything. But that's all changing now!"

As she spoke, Máire's voice grew in volume and

fury. Sixteen years of fearing, dreaming, regretting, wondering, ruminating, and longing burst forth in a venomous tirade against the man she blamed for destroying her life in Ætheria and ripping her son from her. She'd often thought about what she'd say to Stan Leif if she had the chance. Now everything was trying to come out at once, but she found her voice choking in her rage.

Gasping for breath, Máire rushed to the cabinet where Stan had been standing when they'd entered and ripped it open. The ACF scouts gasped at the sight of hundreds of oxygen canisters stacked from the floor to the ten-foot-tall ceiling. If they'd been harboring any doubts about the truth of Máire's story, those vanished as she moved down the wall pulling open cabinet after cabinet, revealing thousands more. Just in this room alone, there were enough canisters for everyone in Ætheria—all ten thousand. The scouts shook their heads—not so much in disbelief as in growing anger at the

Head Ductor from keeping all of this from his people. Why?

With all of the cabinets opened, Máire, wheezing from the effort, turned and faced Stan, who had rushed over and begun closing the cabinets after her.

"No!" she shouted yanking an oxygen tank from its storage. "Leave them open! Ætheria needs to know!"

With that, she hurled the canister like a football across the room—straight toward Stan's amphibian-like face. He ducked the attack. The ACF jerked their weapons up, preparing for a fight. The ten-pound tank smacked into a row of canisters' nozzles, snapping off six or seven as it fell to the ground. With a machine gun-like *Pop! Pop! Pop! Pop! Pop! Pop!* the nozzles shot across the room like bullets, ricocheting off another wall of canisters and sending a few more nozzles popping. As the projectiles flew about, the ACF, Rex, and Stan ducked and covered their heads. Only Máire remained erect, her eyes glued on her ex-husband.

No sooner had the nozzles erupted from the pressurized containers than a chorus of high-pitched hissing filled the room, making it difficult to speak. From each damaged canister, a yard-long geyser of misty-looking gas flowed out with the power of small rocket boosters. The room was filling with pure oxygen.

"You see!" Máire said when the ricocheting nozzles had settled to the ground. She pointed to the gas. "Oxygen! Just open some more and in a few seconds you'll all be able to feel the difference!"

To make her point, Máire started twisting frantically at the stored canisters' nozzles, releasing even more oxygen in the room.

As she did this, Rex quickly felt the effect. Just as when his SCRM had been ripped off on Cthonia, his lungs filled to capacity, and a vivifying life force flowed through every pore of his body. He felt stronger, more alert, more lucid. He looked around at the Ætherians. From the glint in their eyes, he saw they too were feeling the same thing. Their *bodies* now told them that the Head Ductor and all of Ætheria were a lie. They felt it in their organs and in every cell of their bodies.

At this point, Stan reacted. With a shriek, his face went purple with rage and panic, and he rushed up to the broken canisters. Like the boy damming the cracked dike with his fingers, he desperately pushed his fingers against the different oxygen geysers. Their blast was too powerful. When he approached his hand, the gas blew it back. He even tried to push his whole body against the line of snapped canisters. All this did was to cause the oxygen to burst out from his sides. From behind, he looked like he was being fried on top of some sort of bizarre grill, the gas being the steam let out by his frying flesh.

A violent knock at the door made the ACF and Rex jump.

"Head Ductor?" the guard's muffled voice came from outside. "Is everything okay? We're coming in."

"Block the door!" Ama shouted to the ACF scouts who had stationed themselves by the double doors. The two looked around frantically. The door could not be locked from the inside, but it had two large handles that might work like a latch that they could jam. One of them looked toward the meeting table and rushed to one of the wooden chairs. Holstering his Stær gun, he lifted the chair above his head and slammed it onto the floor, smashing it into four pieces. He grabbed the remains of one of the legs and rushed back to the door. He jammed the leg through the handles, forming an improvised lock. The two then gripped both sides of the wood to keep it from sliding out in either direction.

The pounding at the door became more intense. The guard started to shout something, but Rex had the impression he was shouting in a different direction. Was he calling for reinforcements? Ama had said only about fifty ACF had remained in Ætheria, but what if they all came now? Rex's muscles tensed and his heartbeat sped. He looked at his mother, who had stopped opening up oxygen tanks and was stepping toward Stan . . . his father.

By now, Rex could feel nothing but pure oxygen in the room. He also had the sense that the air had become thicker, as if the room were becoming pressurized like the airship. Every breath brought energy and clarity.

"You're finished," Máire said, looking Stan in the eye. "The ACF are telling everyone right now. They'll know. But you can still do the right thing. Give up . . . let go of this power you've always wanted. Come down to Cthonia, and let's see what we can do. There's no reason this has to end in tragedy. But our time—your time—on this vertical world is over."

Stan took a few tentative steps toward her and glanced around at the others, as if trying to decide what to do. His hands were trembling. He looked as if he might cry. Rex even thought he saw his dad's lower lip quivering.

"No," Stan said, his voice calmer. "It's *not* over.

Why would you say that?" He looked around at the thousands of exposed oxygen tanks. "All I have to do is give these out to everyone. That's why I've been keeping them . . . I even told you that way back when. I only ever did this for the good of the people of Ætheria. They need me. And only I can save them." His chest heaved with each breath. Rex wondered if he too was feeling the effects of the oxygen. Normally he would be wearing one on his back, but for some reason when they came in, he wasn't. Instead, he'd been huffing oxygen from the canisters like a drug addict.

Máire kept her eyes on Stan as she considered his words. Ten seconds passed. The hissing continued around them as the room became saturated with oxygen. She shook her head and looked to Rex. Her eyes sparkled with determination. She looked back to Stan.

"You've lost," she said. "You've lost your mind. We can't do anything to help you. If you want to sink with this place, then sink. But everyone knows the truth now. And they've been hearing everything we've been saying thanks to the Trackers in here that are picking it all up."

A panicked expression crossed Stan's face when she mentioned this. His beady eyes darted across the Ætherians' wrists. How could he have not thought about the Trackers? How could he have not realized that everything they'd said had been transmitted back to Bernuac HQ?

He looked back at Máire and clenched his fists. Every muscle in his face tightened.

"You . . . " he seethed. "You've only ever wanted to destroy me. First *him*." He nodded derisively toward Rex. "You wanted people to know he was mine and show everyone how weak I was. Then he starts stirring up trouble here, so much so I can't have him get strong and learn the truth about me. So I force him into the ACF—into what would be a suicide mission. But he survived! And he found you! And now, like some Greek tragedy, both of you are back. But you'll see: Fate's not in charge here. I am!"

In one explosive movement, Stan leapt forward like the frog he so resembled. As he flew through the air, he reached his hands out for Máire's throat.

"Mom!" Rex screamed and lunged out at his father.

Just before the three collided at the head of the round table, Ama and Pace fired their Stær guns at the Head Ductor. With two quick pops, electric sparks burst from their weapons and into the oxygen-filled room.

EPILOGUE
Two Hundred Years Later

It was a sunny day in Cthonia. A cool breeze blew in from the west, making the knee-high grass ebb and flow in waves. The cherry trees had just come into bloom, filling the air with pollen and white petals that wafted from their branches like snowflakes.

Six miles up, the hazy remains of the Ætherian archipelago glistened in the sunlight. Over the past two hundred years, the islands, no longer maintained, had begun to crumble bit by bit. This made it dangerous for anyone to wander into what had become known as the Ætherian Forest—a network of hundreds of stratoneum struts and rusting guy wires that once held up a stratospheric civilization of several thousand people. When chunks of the man-made islands fell, they struck the ground at nearly two hundred miles per hour. A few people had been killed by falling debris when the unified Ætherians and Cthonians had first begun rebuilding their world near their new water source in the caves of the rocky outcropping nearby. Since then, the Ætherian Forest was off-limits.

But this didn't prevent Cthonia's children from lying as near as they could to the first guy wires and staring up in wonder at the lost civilization. The children—some tall and paler, some short and darker, some in between in height and skin tone— would imagine how it could've been that people could actually live so high up. As they squinted into the sunlight at the darkened bottoms of the islands, generations of children would bounce questions off of each other—questions inspired by the legends and stories told to them by their parents about generations long past.

"Is it warm up there?"

"What's the weather like?"

"How did they get from island to island?"

"How did they get water?"

"Look there, in the middle. It looks like there used to be an island, but the poles just stop. You see? They look bent at the top. I wonder why?"

"Why did they even build those things in the first place?"

"What do you think it was like to live up there?"

Usually, the children didn't hang around long before running off to play Cthonians and Ætherians—a game that was little more than tag. By now, the word "Ætherian" meant little to them, as there were no Ætherians any more, only Cthonians. The last true Ætherians, so went the story, had all come down two centuries before and settled in the cave-filled outcroppings. When the Cthonians had arrived looking for water, the two peoples blended and settled together, making differences between them a thing of legends, myths, and nighttime stories.

But sometimes, just sometimes, the children didn't listen to their parents' warnings to stay out of the forest. Sometimes they jumped the fence that had been built around the archipelago's perimeter to keep people out. Sometimes they disappeared inside, where the untended grass had grown high enough for them to disappear from each other, making Cthonians and Ætherians even more exciting.

And sometimes, but only rarely, in the middle of a heated game, would one of the children stumble across a small, marble marker that had been placed in the middle of the forest, directly under the missing island. The monument was one foot high and three feet square. From this distance it looked like a short table. But as they got nearer, an engraved inscription became clear:

In honored memory of
Máire and Rex Himmel, mother and son,
who through their courage brought our two
worlds together as one new family,
but who sacrificed all by confronting the
tyrannical leader of Ætheria.
Their lives were sadly extinguished in the
final explosion of the War for Oxygen.
May they rest in peace.